It's all fun and

"OK, guys, here's a scorecard for the resolution game," Maria said at lunch the next day. "Everybody gets one."

Elizabeth peered at the paper. There were three columns. The first was labeled Name, the second Resolution, and the third Kill.

"Kill? What's this mean?" she asked, tapping her finger on the third column.

Amy burst into a grin. "I was just thinking. I'd like to be supportive of most of these resolutions. Like Maria's and yours. But there's a certain person who I don't want to be supportive of at all," she said. "There's a certain person I'm going to try to get out of the game just as soon as possible." Her eyes gleamed.

"A certain person who is rude, obnoxious, self-centered, and a lot of other things, but I ran out of adjectives," Maria went on.

Elizabeth took a quick look at the Unicorner, the table where the Unicorns usually sat. "Janet?" she whispered.

"Got it in one," Maria said, smiling.

Amy made a gun out of her forefinger and thumb and pointed it at Janet. "Zap!"

Visit the Official Sweet Valley Web Site on the Internet at:

http://www.sweetvalley.com

SWEET VALLEY TWINS

If Looks Could Kill

Written by
Jamie Suzanne

Created by
FRANCINE PASCAL

BANTAM BOOKS
NEW YORK · TORONTO · LONDON · SYDNEY · AUCKLAND

Suy

To Ben Markowitz, Johnny's friend

RL 4, 008-012

IF LOOKS COULD KILL
A Bantam Book / January 1998

*Sweet Valley High® and Sweet Valley Twins® are
registered trademarks of Francine Pascal.*

Conceived by Francine Pascal.

*Produced by Daniel Weiss Associates, Inc.
33 West 17th Street
New York, NY 10011.*

Cover art by Bruce Emmett.

ISBN: 0-553-48443-5

Published simultaneously in the United States and Canada

*Bantam Books are published by Bantam Books, a division of Bantam
Doubleday Dell Publishing Group, Inc. Its trademark, consisting of the
words "Bantam Books" and the portrayal of a rooster, is Registered in the
U.S. Patent and Trademark Office and in other countries. Marca
Registrada. Bantam Books, 1540 Broadway, New York, New York 10036.*

PRINTED IN THE UNITED STATES OF AMERICA

OPM   0 9 8 7 6 5 4 3 2 1

One

"Now this one," Jessica Wakefield proclaimed, "is very cool."

She slid the purple-and-gold makeup bag off the pharmacy shelf. "Check out the compartments," she told her sister, Elizabeth. "There must be a million of them."

"Why do you need so many compartments when you don't have that much makeup?" Elizabeth asked, stifling a yawn. "Come on, Jess, let's hit the bookstore. I need some more information about rocks and minerals."

Jessica made a face. She'd heard enough about her sister's rock-and-mineral collection during the last week to last a lifetime. Several lifetimes, in fact. Of all the stupid hobbies to have . . . "Wait a second, Lizzie," she directed, examining the makeup bag critically. "I know I don't have tons of makeup *yet*, but I'll get more. You wouldn't expect me to keep my cosmetics in a shoe box or something, would you?" She curled her lip in disgust.

"I keep my rock-and-mineral collection in a shoe box," Elizabeth answered.

"Yeah, well, you would." She looked longingly at the bag. *No doubt about it*, Jessica thought. *This bag would be perfect.* "See, the compartments are even padded. Not that *you* would care anything about that."

The twins, twelve years old and in the sixth grade at Sweet Valley Middle School, were spending the afternoon of New Year's Eve at the mall. Jessica fingered the outside of the makeup bag. "Anyway," she argued, "I really need a bag like this. I'm planning to use mascara and lip gloss and everything for Lila's big party." Jessica's friend Lila Fowler was hosting a school party at her mansion that night, and Jessica was determined to make a splash. She frowned at her sister. "You're planning to dress up too, I hope?"

Showing up in jeans and a T-shirt would be typical Elizabeth, she decided. Not that her twin lacked a sense of style. No. It was just that Elizabeth wasn't that interested in fashion. Take the stupid little stone she wore on a pendant around her neck. A diamond or an emerald or even a topaz would be pretty cool, but *no*—this was just a *rock*. A plain old ordinary reddish rock. Big fat hairy deal.

"Dress up?" Elizabeth considered. "Oh, I don't know. Maybe . . ."

Jessica shook her head.

On the outside the twins were completely identical. Each girl had long blond hair and greenish blue eyes. They even showed a dimple in the same cheek when they smiled.

But on the inside they were different as could be. Jessica lived for fashion, friends, and parties. She was a member of the Unicorn Club, which was made up of the most popular girls at Sweet Valley Middle School. She considered herself to be mature and sophisticated. Elizabeth, on the other hand, was thoughtful and a serious student. She preferred to spend time with a few close friends, and her main interests were reading and writing, and lately her rock-and-mineral collection.

Despite their differences the twins were usually best friends. But Jessica had to admit that they'd been around each other too much over vacation. Everything about Elizabeth was becoming very irritating. Her lack of fashion sense. Her lack of interest in makeup. Her rock-and-mineral collection . . .

"Actually—" Elizabeth reached for a bag herself. "I might just get one of these."

"You?" Jessica stared at her sister in surprise. As far as she knew, one tube of lip balm was the extent of Elizabeth's makeup. "What are you going to do—put your hair ribbons in it?"

Elizabeth hefted the bag experimentally. "No," she said. "My rocks and minerals. With all the compartments I could make sure they don't bump into each other when I carry them around."

Jessica sighed. *It figures.* "Oh, there's nothing worse than when your rocks and minerals bump into each other," she remarked sarcastically. "I hate it when that happens."

"So do I," Elizabeth agreed. "They can damage each other pretty badly. Especially if you put rocks together that are of different hardnesses. Like talc and granite—one of them starts chipping the other one and it's just a mess."

Jessica couldn't possibly have cared less. "*This* bag is for makeup," she said frostily.

Elizabeth shrugged. "Is there a law that you can't use it for rocks and minerals?"

Jessica glowered at her sister. *Well, there should be.* Honestly, Elizabeth had a way of ruining everything. Jessica could just see her Unicorn friends now, poking fun at her if Elizabeth showed up at school with a bag just like Jessica's own. "*Oh, cool, Jessica!*" Ellen Riteman would say in a mocking voice. "*Did you take up rock collecting too?*" And Lila would add, "*It must run in the family.*" And Janet Howell, the president of the club, would glare at Jessica and say, "*If you're going to collect rocks, Jessica, we'll have to reconsider your membership in this club. . . ."* "Thanks a lot, Lizzie," she muttered.

Elizabeth glanced up. "Did you say something?"

"Forget it!" Angrily Jessica shoved the makeup bag back onto the shelf. There was no way she could buy it now. From now on, anytime Jessica looked at one of these she'd see rocks, not makeup.

"Oooh, thirty-nine ninety-five," Elizabeth said, wincing. She set the makeup bag neatly on the shelf. "Too much. I guess my collection will have to stay in that shoe box a little longer. Come on, Jess, let's go."

Jessica allowed her sister to pull her away from the makeup counter.

Still, she couldn't help thinking that Elizabeth's biggest rock collection consisted of the rocks in her head.

"Hey, Joe! Hold on a minute, OK? I want to see this."

Steven Wakefield, the twins' older brother, paused outside the electronics store at the mall and peered through the window at the wide-screen TV. "I didn't know it was three-thirty already," he remarked. "Look, Phyllis Hartley's on."

Steven's friend Joe Howell snorted. "Since when have you been such a big Phyllis Hartley fan?"

"Since this week." Steven leaned closer. The popular talk show hostess was looking confidently at the camera and speaking into a handheld microphone. Every one of her hairs was in place. Automatically

Steven reached up to pat down his own wavy dark hair. "I haven't missed a show since school let out. Did you see the one where the guests were talking about their worst dates ever? It was so cool."

Joe yawned lazily. "Not exactly."

"They interviewed a woman, OK?" Steven went on. "This guy had invited her out for dinner and a movie, but before the movie he said he had to pick something up from the office and asked if she wanted to see where he worked. So she was, like, no problemo." He stared at the screen. Phyllis was flashing the audience a dazzling grin, showing all seventy-nine of her perfect teeth. "So they ate Chinese and went to his office," he continued, "only it turned out the guy was a scientist and there were all these dead frogs lying around the lab and he'd been dissecting them—"

"And she threw up," Joe said. "Sweet-and-sour barf all over the frogs."

Steven frowned. "How did you know?" He shifted his eyes from the screen and stared at his friend in surprise.

Joe tapped his forehead. "Some people got the looks, some people got the brains," he intoned. "And I got 'em both."

"I'll tell you what you've got—you've *got* to get over yourself," Steven scoffed. "Seriously, how'd you know?" He smiled to himself, remembering the end of the show. Phyllis had grinned her humongous grin and opened the secret door to the stage, and the frog guy himself had come walking out, and the woman's jaw had hung open, like, three *feet*, and—

"But the coolest part," Joe said, "was when they got the scientist to appear on the show." He gave Steven a knowing grin. "I figure they'll probably get married now. As long as they remember not to eat frogs' legs at the wedding."

"You did too watch that show," Steven said accusingly. "You lied."

Joe laughed. "*I* didn't watch the show. My sister, *Janet*, watched the show. I just happened to be in the room." He narrowed his eyes. "I can't believe you've been watching *Phyllis Hartley* all *week*. Man, what a stupid program."

"It's no dumber than lots of other stuff that's on nowadays," Steven said defensively.

"Like what?" Joe challenged.

"Like—" Steven searched his mind. "Like *Sweetie Pie and the Honeybunch Gang*," he said, naming a cartoon show he'd seen last Saturday while channel surfing. It was on after his favorite, *Ratshark*. "Not that I watch that or anything," he added hastily as Joe's lips curled into a mocking grin. "Not really. I just ran into it once or twice and—I mean, I saw the ads and . . ." His voice trailed off. Something told him he was just getting himself in deeper.

"I guess you'll watch anything, huh?" Joe asked. "How about *Celebrity Ping-Pong*?"

"I don't watch *Celebrity Ping-Pong,*" Steven scoffed. *Except last week when Johnny Buck beat that babe from* Homicide Plus! *. . . but that was a really good episode!* "What kind of guy do you think I am?"

All the same, Steven felt a twinge of guilt. He *had* been watching a lot of television during vacation. Still, what else was a guy supposed to do with himself? Basketball practice had stopped while school was out, and the beach volleyball courts had been taken over by snotty college kids who were too good for a high-school freshman like him anyway, and he and his girlfriend, Cathy, were sort of on the outs. And though there was this new girl in town, this Patty Weinstein or Weinville or something, he hadn't gotten around to asking her out yet.

And it wasn't like there was anything else to *do* in Sweet Valley.

So, since the cable company was nice enough to give them almost a hundred channels, it would be a shame to let them go to waste. His eyes flicked back up to the TV screen.

"Well, suit yourself." Joe shrugged. "I'm heading to Casey's for a sundae. You coming, or are you going to stand and gawk at Phyllis Hartley all day instead?"

Steven took a deep breath. Phyllis was holding the microphone out to a nervous-looking man wearing a lumberjack shirt. There was an expression of deep *caring* on her face.

"Wakefield!" Joe sounded annoyed.

Phyllis nodded sympathetically. The camera panned the audience. Steven leaned against the doorway.

"Order for me," he said. "I'll be there in a few minutes, OK?"

"I know you, don't I? Both of you?"

Elizabeth blinked in surprise as she and Jessica walked out of the pharmacy. A good-looking dark-haired boy was standing in the doorway. "One of you is Elizabeth," he said with an engaging grin, "and the other one's Jessica, but I can't tell which is which."

"I'm Jessica," Jessica said quickly, stepping in front of Elizabeth. "How are you doing, Eric?"

It's Eric Weinberg. Elizabeth sucked in her breath. Eric was new to Sweet Valley Middle School. He had joined the sixth grade at the beginning of December, and Elizabeth thought he was kind of cute. "Hi, Eric," she said, stepping around Jessica. "I'm Elizabeth. Um—" She flashed him a bright smile, trying to think of something to say. "Well, fancy meeting you here!"

"He *lives* in Sweet Valley, duh," Jessica observed pointedly. She stepped back around Elizabeth. "It's easy to tell us apart, Eric. Just remember, I'm the pretty one."

"Very funny." Elizabeth rolled her eyes. There wasn't room to step around Jessica again, so she edged forward instead, shoving her twin gently to one side. Pushing Jessica made her feel a little guilty, but only a little. Most of the time her sister was pretty easy to get along with, but somehow this week she'd turned into—well, into somebody who was not very easy to get along with. "What brings you to the mall today?"

Eric made a face. "I'm here with my sister, Patty. She's a freshman at Sweet Valley High School." He jerked his thumb over his shoulder. "We're going to meet at Casey's in a few minutes. Have you guys ever eaten at Casey's?"

"Have I eaten at Casey's?" Jessica laid a hand on Eric's shoulder. "Eric, you're talking to the expert on Casey's ice cream. Me and my friends are there almost every single day of the week."

"Oh, you are not," Elizabeth said crossly, fingering her pendant the way she often did when she was annoyed. The red polished stone sometimes seemed to calm her down. She didn't know why she was finding Jessica so obnoxious right now. Maybe it was the way Jessica was acting as if she owned Eric. The hand on his shoulder and all that stuff . . . "I go to Casey's as much as you do, and I'm not there every day."

"Well, I would go if I was allowed to," Jessica said smoothly. "So, um, how do you like it here in Sweet Valley?"

"I like it!" Eric jammed his hands into his pockets and grinned from one girl to the other.

"Sweet Valley's a cool place. There's the beach, the mountains, everything. And the people seem friendly."

"Oh, we're *very* friendly around here," Jessica assured him.

"We are," Elizabeth chimed in, not about to let her sister be the only friendly one. She tried to wiggle closer but was blocked by Jessica's hip.

"We're so friendly that, in fact—" Jessica broke off. "Um, Elizabeth, what day is Lila's party?"

"Lila's party?" Elizabeth frowned. "You know perfectly well when. Tonight. New Year's Eve."

"Oh, New Year's *Eve*," Jessica murmured lazily. She fluttered her eyelashes at Eric, and Elizabeth felt a sudden pang of jealousy. Eric was looking as if he liked Jessica, really *liked* her. . . . "I get so busy, sometimes I can't keep track. Luckily my sister helps out. She's got a wonderful memory. Too bad she isn't invited to as many parties as—" She paused. "Well, anyway!"

"What are you talking about?" Elizabeth narrowed her eyes. "I get invited to—"

"As I was saying, Eric," Jessica interrupted, "are you coming to the party tonight? It's at my best friend Lila Fowler's house, I mean *mansion*, and lots of kids will be there." She backed up a step, pushing Elizabeth against the doorway.

Eric grinned at Jessica. Elizabeth swallowed hard. Was it her imagination, or did the grin last just a little longer than it needed to? "Oh, the party! Right! You'll be there?"

Elizabeth decided she'd better speak up before Eric forgot about her completely. "*Both* of us will be there," she said over her sister's shoulder, laughing brightly in a way that she hoped didn't sound jealous at all. "Lila is Jessica's friend, but everybody's coming. You'll know a ton of people."

"Lila's great that way," Jessica said with a smile. "She doesn't ever like to leave anybody out."

Yeah, right, Elizabeth thought sourly. Lila was one of the most exclusive people she'd ever known. The only reason other kids were invited at all was that the party was sort of a school event. The student government was paying for decorations and stuff. "We, um, hope to see you there, Eric," she said, quickly stepping around Jessica. *Ha.* Now she was in front of her twin again.

"Hey!" Eric bent forward. "Is that what I think it is?" he asked curiously.

"Is what what you think it is?" Jessica asked impatiently. She grabbed Elizabeth's shoulder and tugged.

"This?" Elizabeth held her ground and fingered her pendant. "It's, um, a rock. Polished. My favorite. It's called—"

"Agate," Eric interrupted. "It's agate, isn't it?"

Elizabeth's hand flew to her mouth, and her heart beat furiously in her chest. "How did you know?"

"Oh, I'm a rock collector from way back," Eric

said, his brown eyes sparkling. "I got my first quartz crystals when I was maybe three, and my collection's been growing ever since. I have seventeen different kinds of basalt and some really cool strips of mica and—" He grinned, looking embarrassed. "So, um, do you like rocks too?"

Elizabeth couldn't hold back a smile. "You could say that."

"Awesome!" Eric flashed her a thumbs-up signal. "Do you specialize in something? And where's a good place around here to go prospecting?"

"Getting back to what we were *talking* about—" Jessica's voice boomed from behind Elizabeth.

"Later, Jessica," Elizabeth said, not bothering to turn around. Gently she rested her hand on Eric's shoulder. "Can't you see that *Eric* and I are having a conversation?"

Two

Joe Howell scooped the maraschino cherry off his sundae and dropped it neatly into his napkin. He'd forgotten to ask for the sundae without the cherry again. Oh, well. He shoved a huge spoonful of whipped cream into his mouth and slurped it down. *Yum.* There was nothing like whipped cream on a Super Sundae from Casey's.

He stole a quick look at the sundae across the table from him. Steven Wakefield's sundae, which Joe had so *kindly* ordered for his TV-watching friend. Which was beginning to melt. A puddle of chocolate ice cream was forming at the bottom of the silver cup.

Slowly he leaned forward. Wakefield would never know. If he ever even showed up. No point in letting the sundae go to waste anyhow. Joe filled his spoon with melted ice cream and darted it quickly into his mouth. *Dee-licious*.

"There you are, Patty!" A voice came from the booth next to Joe, and he swiveled his head to see who was talking. A dark-haired kid was sitting upright in the booth, a menu in his hands. "I've been waiting forever."

"Sorry," a girl murmured. "I got tied up at the bookstore. The kid waiting on me was *really* slow."

Patty? Joe scratched his head and swiveled the other way to see her better. *Patty*. She looked kind of familiar. From school, maybe? He blinked. One thing was for sure, she was awfully good-looking. Dark brown hair, cut short and pulled back from her face with a bright red headband. Dark brown eyes and a bright smile. *Whoa!* Joe sat up straighter. Whoever Patty was, she was worth knowing.

But what was with the boyfriend across from her? He looked like a *kid*. Younger even than his little sister, Janet.

"What'd you buy?" The kid handed Patty a menu.

"Oh, this book." Patty wiped her forehead. "Some collection of short stories that they make all the freshmen read here."

Freshmen. Joe narrowed his eyes. *Yeah*. Now he recognized Patty. She was the new kid in the English class that met right after his. He'd noticed her before, but not *noticed* her exactly. Which was a shame, since she certainly seemed to be worth noticing. And not just in the looks department either. She seemed really cheerful and friendly.

"What're you having?" the kid asked. "The Super Sundae looks good."

Not that you could finish it, you twerp. Joe leaned closer, hoping that no one would think he was staring.

Patty smiled. "Here's all the money Mom gave us," she told him, and pulled a few bills from her purse. "It'll cover two basic sundaes. If you want more, you'd better have brought along your own money."

"Aww, man . . ." The boy looked crestfallen. "Bummer."

"It's OK, Eric," Patty said kindly. "Next time. What do you think—hot fudge or butterscotch?"

Brother and sister, Joe thought, oddly relieved. The kid was Patty's brother, that was all. He cleared his throat. "Um—if you don't mind my butting in," he said, hanging over the rail that separated the booths, "I highly recommend the hot fudge."

Patty looked up, a flash of recognition in her eyes. "Have we met?"

"Probably," Joe said in a voice that was squeakier than he'd intended. "I'm in your year at school." He extended a hand. "Joe. Howell, that is."

"Pleased to meet you, Joe," Patty said. Gravely she shook his hand. "I'm Patty Weinberg. And this is Eric. My so-called brother," she said with a smile. "Nice to meet you."

"Nice to meet *you.*" Joe paused awkwardly. Now what? It was strange how a really cool dude like himself sometimes had trouble talking to girls. *"So, like, you want to go out sometime?"* seemed a little, well, forward. Classes? Sports? He swallowed and all at once decided that he was just too . . . shy. "Hot fudge," he said instead, waving his finger in the air. "Remember, you heard it here first."

"Thanks!" Patty grinned. "I'll keep it in mind. See you around, Joe." She returned to her menu.

Duh! Joe wanted to slap himself on the side of the head. *How could this conversation be over? It had just started!* He wet his lips. "Of course, um, the butterscotch is pretty decent too," he said, but his voice sounded froggy. "I mean—"

"Huh?" Patty frowned and looked up.

Joe sighed. "Never mind," he said, and dug back into his sundae.

"Hey, Howell!" Steven slid into the seat opposite Joe. "Thanks for ordering for me. Sorry I'm late. Know what Phyllis was talking about today?"

Joe rolled his eyes. *"Phyllis?" Give me a break!* "What?" he asked, trying to sound as bored as possible. Inside he was still kicking himself over his missed opportunity with Patty.

"It was so cool," Steven said, thrusting a spoon-ful of melted ice cream into his mouth. "Get this title: 'Losers Who Are Afraid to Ask Women Out.'" Something trickled down his chin. "They had these four guys on, see, and they were all, like, passion-ately in love with some woman or other and they *would not* ask them out. The women, I mean." He paused for breath and stuck his spoon back into the sundae. "And these women, they were truly babes. They showed their pictures and everything."

Joe looked up at the ceiling and blew out a burst of air. *"Losers Who Are Afraid to Ask Women Out." Great.* He was suddenly aware of Patty sitting one booth over. *Very* aware. Very, very, *very* aware. "Gee, I wonder where they get people for shows like that," he said, shaking his head as if he himself never had that problem.

"Who knows?" Steven gestured with his spoon. "And get this. They called up one of the women and described the man to her, and she said—"

"You mean to tell me you watched that whole show straight through?" Joe demanded.

Steven squirmed. "Well, that was just the first half. The second half was about people who treat their pets better than their children. It was a rerun, so I bagged it. Saw it last spring. Well, actually . . ." He stirred the ice in his water glass, looking uncomfortable. "I watched the first few minutes of that part too."

Joe shook his head sadly. "Man, you know what you are? You're a television addict."

"No way," Steven protested feebly. "I can take it or leave it. I happen to *like* TV, that's all. It's educational and everything." He slurped up more ice cream. "You learn a lot from watching shows like *Phyllis*. But if I wanted to stop watching right this minute, I could." He snapped his fingers. "Poof!"

Joe snorted. "You *wish*. I bet you couldn't not watch for the rest of vacation."

"I could," Steven said virtuously. "If I wanted to. I just don't want to. I bet you couldn't cut out Casey's Super Sundaes for the rest of vacation."

"That's different," Joe said. He was sure he could skip Super Sundaes, probably even skip coming to Casey's. If he had to. Almost sure anyway. "Casey's isn't the same as TV."

"Very observant," Steven said. He raised his water glass to his lips—and froze. "Hey! Patty!"

Startled, Joe looked to the next booth. Patty Weinberg was just setting down her spoon. "Hi, Steven," she said with a warm smile. "How are you?"

"Good," Steven said, grinning a chocolate-stained grin. "How about you and me do something together sometime, huh? You know, go to my house to watch *Phyllis Hartley* or something? Or I guess we could do something else if you don't like TV."

"Hmm!" Patty nodded slowly. "That might be fun, Steven. Call me and we'll see if we can work out a time, OK?"

"You got it," Steven said with a wink. He turned back to Joe. "No way Phyllis could get *me* on her show!" he said, sticking out his chest.

Joe sighed. Much as he hated to admit it, Steven was way ahead of him in the girl department. "No way," he agreed, wishing he had just a few ounces more courage.

Yup, hitting the big time. Steven grinned and opened the door to his house. "I'm home!" he yelled. *Did I totally impress Patty Weinberg or what?* he thought. He'd talked to Patty a few times at school since she'd moved to Sweet Valley, but this was different. He'd practically invited her on a real date.

"Hi, Steven!" his mother called from the dining room. "How was the mall?"

"Great!" Steven loped into the living room and seized the remote control. Yes, sirree, an evening of television watching with the girl of his dreams was just the ticket. He could see Patty curled against his shoulder right now, the two of them sitting on the couch, staring together at the flickering light of some really romantic show like *Shark Attack!* They'd hold hands and maybe even kiss. During the commercials, of course. He aimed the remote at the TV set and clicked the on button.

The picture came to life. A small furry animal stared into the camera, white whiskers drooping sadly down its face. A glowing 89 appeared in the upper-left corner of the screen.

Channel 89. Hmm. Steven frowned. He'd thought he had the channels all memorized, but maybe not.

"Steven, are you watching TV again?" Mrs. Wakefield called from the next room.

"Only for a while, Mom," Steven yelled back. It was like he'd told Howell. He could take TV or leave it. He hit the volume control and the sound came on. "Ah, the raccoon!" a voice said happily. "Few animals are as well adapted to the urban environment as this little rascal."

Besides, Steven told himself, *if I didn't watch TV, I'd miss great shows like this.*

Whatever it was.

With a contented sigh he propped his feet on the coffee table and leaned back among the couch pillows.

"Will you just give it *up*, Lizzie?" Jessica snarled. Setting her jaw, she shoved open the door of their house. For the last hour at *least*, Elizabeth had been going on and on about how much Eric Weinberg liked *her* when it was just so clear that Eric liked *Jessica* instead. Any fool could see that. She marched through the doorway, giving the door a hard push so it would fly into her sister's face. "Give it a rest, OK?"

"You're just jealous." Elizabeth's voice was furious. "You've been jealous ever since Eric noticed my pendant. Can *I* help it if you're just not *interesting* to him?"

"Same old, same old." Jessica shrugged, feeling terribly angry at her sister. It seemed as if she'd been feeling this way an awful lot lately. "If you can't think of anything *new* to say, Elizabeth—"

"*You're* the one who needs to—" Elizabeth started.

"You're such a *baby*." Jessica folded her arms. She was dimly aware of the noise of the television in the living room, tuned to a show she didn't recognize. She had to raise her voice to be heard. "If you had ever had a *real* boyfriend—"

"Quiet!" Steven's voice boomed from the living room. "I can't hear the Pet Channel!"

"You be quiet!" the twins shouted in unison.

"Girls!" Their mother appeared around the corner, an envelope in her hand and an angry look on her face. "What on earth is going on?"

Elizabeth swallowed hard. "Um—not much, Mom."

"Nothing we can't handle," Jessica added, glaring at her sister. "If this clown here didn't think she was the greatest thing since—"

"If *you* didn't think you were the center of the universe!" Elizabeth broke in.

"Hey!" Jessica bit her lip. "*I'm* not the one who—"

"Girls!" Mrs. Wakefield's eyes flashed, and the twins were quiet. "This is a letter from your aunt Nancy and uncle Kirk."

"Aunt Nancy?" Jessica blinked. Aunt Nancy was one of her very favorite relatives. Her older daughter, Robin, was the same age as the twins and was one of their best friends. "What does she say?"

Mrs. Wakefield consulted the letter. "They *were* writing to invite you two and Steven to their ski condo for spring break."

"Skiing over break!" Jessica's eyes lit up. "I can't wait!"

"What do you mean—*were?*" Elizabeth asked cautiously.

"Yes!" the television blared in the background. "Brush your pet guinea pig with WAVE!, the all-new antidandruff shampoo that leaves no gritty residue whatsoever!"

"Were," Mrs. Wakefield said sternly. "You two are usually such good friends. But this week's been—different. You've been fighting so much lately, I'm not sure I can trust you to go without us. And this argument clinches it." She folded the letter and thrust it into her pocket. "Steven can go. But as for the two of you—"

She looked meaningfully from one girl to the other. Jessica held her breath in dismay. Her mother couldn't . . . wouldn't . . . surely not . . .

"You're not mature enough," Mrs. Wakefield said with finality. "We're keeping you home."

Three

"Now look what you did," Elizabeth said accusingly. In her heart of hearts she knew that she had been just as much at fault as Jessica—well, almost as much anyway—but she couldn't resist blaming her sister. She folded her arms and leaned against the entryway. "If you hadn't been so totally *obnoxious*—"

"Look who's talking." Jessica set her jaw. "Thanks to you, we're out a trip to the slopes. I hope you can *live* with yourself, *Elizabeth*."

Mrs. Wakefield shook her head. "Exhibit A," she said.

Elizabeth bit back an angry retort to her sister. Her mom was right. The twins weren't exactly showing how mature they were by arguing. "Please, may we go?" she asked. "We won't fight anymore."

"Oh, girls." Mrs. Wakefield sighed. "I've already heard that—"

"But this time it happens to be true!" Jessica argued. She strained to think what good friends she and her sister had been just a week ago. Only a week! It seemed like a month. Ever since vacation had started, they'd been getting on each other's nerves constantly. "I know we've been fighting and stuff, but this is different."

"We mean it this time," Elizabeth remarked.

"Yeah, we really mean it." Jessica was glad to have her twin on her side for a change. "This is a *promise,* Mom."

A sad smile appeared on Mrs. Wakefield's face. "The way you've been acting, you probably couldn't stop arguing for two minutes, let alone—"

"Oh, we could too," Jessica said. "We could stop arguing for two *weeks.*" She glanced at Elizabeth and then dropped her gaze. "One week anyway. At least *I* could."

Elizabeth chose to ignore this last remark. "We could do it, Mom," she insisted, wiping a stray hair out of her face. She couldn't imagine letting her brother go off on the trip without them. "We *really* could."

"Please?" Jessica blinked rapidly.

There was silence.

"Yes, just in time for the New Year!" a Pet Channel commercial boomed out. "Anti-itching powder specially designed for French poodles! Start your dog's new year off right with the gift that gets you out of your pet's hair for good!"

New Year. Jessica ran her tongue lightly along her upper lip. "Actually, Mom," she began, "we, um, wanted to talk to you about, you know, getting along. Since it's New Year's and all. It was going to be our resolution," she lied, making frantic signs at her sister. "Wasn't it, Lizzie?"

"Oh, um, yeah," Elizabeth said, smiling sincerely. "Um, our New Year's resolution. We're going to, er, get along. I know it's been kind of tough living with us lately, but that's going to change. Honest."

"Honest," Jessica echoed her. She raised her hand as if she were taking an oath. "I, Jessica Wakefield, do solemnly swear . . . so how about it?"

Mrs. Wakefield sighed. "You two," she said. "All right. I'll put you on probation. If you can manage till, say, Friday without a single argument . . ." Her voice trailed off.

"A week," Elizabeth repeated. It sounded like an awfully long time, but it was worth a try. Maybe Jessica would break her leg and have to go live in the hospital for a while, and then it would be easy. "So we don't argue for a week, and then?"

"Then you can go skiing with Uncle Kirk and Aunt Nancy," Mrs. Wakefield said. "Not that I expect this is going to happen. A week." She turned toward the living room. "Remember, no fighting means no fighting. None. Zero, zilch. I have spies everywhere."

"No fighting," Elizabeth promised, heaving a sigh of relief.

"No fighting," Jessica echoed her. "Cool. I'm going to call Lila and Janet right away and tell them!" She elbowed Elizabeth out of her way and took the steps to their bedroom two at a time.

"Ow!" Elizabeth grabbed her side and winced. She was about to complain to her sister but caught herself.

No way was she letting Jessica spoil it for her in less than two minutes.

All the same, if her sister was going to keep behaving this way, it promised to be a very long week.

"So let me get this straight, Mom," Steven said, staring at the long-haired guinea pig walking unsteadily across the screen in front of him. "First you say the twins can't come on the ski trip, and then you say they can?" He shook his head. "I mean, it's not like I'm the world's expert on being a parent or anything, but don't you think you ought to stick to your guns? You said no, you mean no. Simple as that."

Besides, it would be tons more fun at the ski condo without his dorky sisters. If he played his cards right, maybe he could even bring Joe or somebody along.

Mrs. Wakefield smiled. "Between you and me, Steven, I doubt very much that their resolution is going to get anywhere." She shuffled through the rest of the afternoon mail. "At least we'll get some peace and quiet out of this."

"Well, you're the boss." Steven stroked his chin thoughtfully. On the TV screen the guinea pig was leaning against a pile of bricks and twitching its nose. "Guinea pig owners must be sure to feed their pets plenty of roughage," the announcer pointed out.

"Darn right," Steven said approvingly. *Whatever roughage is.* He leaned forward to see better.

"Rabbits, on the other hand," the announcer intoned, "thrive on a mixed diet of sunflower seeds, lettuce leaves, and the occasional carrot." The camera cut to a brown rabbit loping into a small child's lap.

"Cool," Steven muttered. *Sunflower seeds. Learn something new every—*

"Steven?" Mrs. Wakefield looked up, a frown on her face. "Why are we watching this show? It's not as though we own a guinea pig or a rabbit."

Steven shrugged. "We could get one now that we know how to take care of them. But I'll switch to something else if you want." He found the channel changer and pressed the down arrow.

The rabbit disappeared. A woman in a bikini took its place. Steven settled back into the couch pillows, watching as the woman ran forward in slow motion across a beach, blowing a whistle frantically, and plunged into the pounding surf. "Hey, awesome," he muttered, his eyes glued to the screen. "A rerun of *Shark Attack!*"

"Oh, Steven." Mrs. Wakefield sighed. "You know I don't approve of—"

"No problem," Steven assured her. He clicked the button once again. Now a girl in a red running suit and a bike helmet was dangling in the air from a rope. Steven squinted. She was throwing basketballs into an oversize bathtub while kids cheered behind her. "Elena's score is now up to twenty-six points!" a man yelled over the din.

Kids' Challenge, that was the name of the show. It wasn't Steven's favorite anymore, he was really too old for it now, but it was still fun to watch once in a while. He remembered the time when the contestants had dived into a pool of mashed potatoes and—

"Steven." Mrs. Wakefield reached for the channel changer. She pressed the off button, and the screen went black.

Steven swallowed hard. The silence was deafening. "What's up, Mom?" he demanded irritably.

Mrs. Wakefield peered into his face. "You've been watching an awful lot of television lately."

Steven reddened. First Joe, now his mom. "Yeah, well," he said. "It's not that big a deal to me. I can, you know, take it or leave it." He stared at the empty screen. Was it his imagination, or could he still hear the cries of the *Kids' Challenge* crowd?

"Really?" Mrs. Wakefield laid a hand on his arm. "If the girls can try a week without fighting, maybe you should consider making a New Year's resolution too."

"Like what?" Steven narrowed his eyes.

"Like giving up television," his mother suggested.

"Giving up television? Cold turkey?" Steven sat up straight, horrified at the idea. "Huh? A man's got to watch the news, doesn't he? Plus all the other important things that are on TV these days. Like the channel with all the really cool science shows—" He searched his mind for other examples.

"And the Pet Channel," Mrs. Wakefield said with a wry smile. "And cartoons."

Steven snorted. "Cartoons are works of art," he argued. "I saw that on a show last week. The guy said it was the only decent form of art anybody's been doing in the last thirty years." Steven hoped that sounded good.

Mrs. Wakefield shook her head. "Are you saying you're not responsible enough to quit watching television?" she asked.

"Me? Well—" Steven scratched his ear. Out of habit he looked at the television screen in front of him. It was kind of strange to see it blank. "Well, if you're talking about responsibility . . ." That kind of put a different spin on things.

"I am." Mrs. Wakefield smiled. "It would be a very mature thing not to watch for a while. I don't know if your sisters could do it. But you're fourteen now, and—well, I think you could manage it. If you put your mind to it."

Steven nodded slowly. No way was his mom going to put him in a not-responsible box with his ugh, sisters. "OK," he said. "You've got yourself a deal. No TV for—a whole week."

"Including videotapes," Mrs. Wakefield put in.

Steven gulped. "Including, um, videotapes."

"I'm proud of you, Steven," Mrs. Wakefield said. "Oh, dear, five o'clock. I really should start dinner."

She stood and walked toward the kitchen.

Five o'clock. Steven bit his lip. His hand moved automatically for the remote. Five o'clock was when *747 Demolition Derby* was on the Monster Trucks Channel. He hadn't missed it all week. What harm would there be if he took just a tiny peek? His thumb was poised above the on button—

No! Steven squeezed his eyes shut tight. The remote fell from his hand, and he willed himself not to pick it up.

He was determined to show everybody just how responsible he could be.

Even if it killed him.

"So what was your argument all about, huh?" Steven asked snottily as Jessica set the table for dinner that night.

Jessica stared at him and blinked. "Argument?" she asked sweetly. "Were we having an argument, Elizabeth?" No way was she breaking her New Year's resolution before the New Year even began.

"Oh, of course not," Elizabeth said, sounding shocked. She yanked open the silverware drawer and handed her twin a few forks. "Here you are, sister *dear.*"

Sister dear. Pardon me while I throw up. Jessica pasted a smile on her face. "We were just having a discussion," she said grandly, waving her hand in the air.

Steven raised his eyebrows. "Oh, a *discussion,*" he said. "Sounded like a pretty wild *discussion.* I could hardly hear the commercial for the gerbil exercise video."

"Oh, it was just an ordinary discussion," Elizabeth said. "Wasn't it, Jessica?"

"Just an ordinary discussion," Jessica repeated, laying the forks around the table. "Nothing *you'd* be interested in." She stepped back to admire her handiwork, not-so-accidentally bumping her brother against the buffet. "So if you don't mind—"

"You can go away and leave us alone," Elizabeth put in.

Steven snorted. "Oh, I don't know," he said meaningfully. "I heard you two talking about some *guy.* Does the name Eric mean anything to you?" He rested his elbow oh-so-casually against the buffet and stared at the twins from under droopy eyelids.

Jessica felt her heart beating faster. But she suspected Steven was only trying to bait her. "Oh, Eric," she said, pretending she'd hardly heard the name. A picture of Eric's handsome face popped into her mind. "Oh, sure. We were talking about a guy named Eric." She laughed lightly, as if Eric were no big deal.

"Oh, Eric," Elizabeth echoed with a shrug. "Eric What's-his-name."

Jessica scowled. As if Elizabeth didn't know his last name backward and forward. Well, Eric was destined to be Jessica's next sort-of boyfriend, that was for sure. The whole idea of Elizabeth and Eric together—it was to laugh. "Whatever," she added airily, doing her best not to look at her sister.

Steven winked at Jessica. "Didn't sound so whatever to me," he said. "Sounded like Mr. Eric's gone and made you two very, very angry at each other."

"Oh, I don't think so," Elizabeth said in a bored tone of voice. She grabbed the salt and pepper shakers and banged them down onto the table. "It was just a discussion is all."

"Like she said," Jessica said, though it pained her to agree with her sister. She thought she knew what Steven was up to. Divide and conquer, that was it. If the twins couldn't keep their resolution and not argue with each other, then Steven would get to go skiing without them.

Which would be a fate worse than death.

"I think Eric liked Elizabeth best," Steven said in a silly voice. "I saw his sister, Patty, at Casey's and kind of, you know, asked her out, and she said he was just gaga over one of you, and she sort of thought it was Elizabeth." He smirked. "So how about it, Jessica? Any *reaction?*"

Jessica could think of several reactions, all right. Such as "Quit lying" and "Cut the jokes." Not to mention "Over my dead body!" But all she said was, "My, my!"

"My, my," Elizabeth echoed, spooning applesauce into a flowered bowl.

Come up with your own lines, Jessica thought irritably. "Eric can like whoever he wants, I guess."

She put her hand to her chest. "I mean, *I* sure don't care who he wants to go out with or anything."

"Me either." Elizabeth clanked the spoon against the inside of the glass jar.

Liar, Jessica thought scornfully. "He's just, you know, a friend."

Steven chewed thoughtfully on his upper lip. "Come to think of it, maybe I got the message wrong." He tapped the side of his head. "Yeah, now I remember. Patty said it the other way around. She said Eric has, like, a major crush on Jessica; that's right. So how about it, Elizabeth? Comments?" His eyes sparkled, and he held out a pretend microphone to Elizabeth.

"He did not," Elizabeth said forcefully, but her eyes darted from Steven's face to Jessica's and back.

"And furthermore," Steven said, "Patty said Eric *used* to like Elizabeth better, but then Jessica came and took him away and—"

"Cut it out, Steven," Jessica interrupted loudly. She smiled at her twin. "Let's just ignore this guy, shall we, Elizabeth?" Reaching across the table, she gave her sister a brief hug around the shoulders.

Elizabeth hesitated, then grinned. "You can't bug us," she added to Steven. "We're sisters, and we love each other."

Gag! Jessica thought. It was all she could do not to roll her eyes.

But she was determined to get along with her sister. No matter what!

Four

"Take a look at *that* kid," Janet Howell said slowly, her eyes glittering. She stared across Lila's ballroom. It was New Year's Eve, and the party was in full swing. "Know what, Jessica? He's kind of cute."

Jessica's heart skipped a beat. Janet was pointing at Eric Weinberg, who had just entered the house. *No duh,* she wanted to say. But Janet was the president of the Unicorn Club, and Jessica knew from long experience that you didn't say that kind of thing to Janet. Not if you wanted to live to tell about it. "He *is* pretty cute, Janet," she murmured. "His name's Eric."

"Eric." Janet raised her eyebrows. "I've seen him around. You know him?"

"Oh, sure," Jessica said quickly. "He and I have been, you know, getting to know each other."

"Sounds like a good idea." Janet picked up a

candy bar from the table and unwrapped it, tearing the paper sharply in two.

Jessica swallowed hard. She did *not* like the look on Janet's face. "He's kind of young for you," she said with a nervous laugh. "You're an eighth-grader; he's only in sixth."

Janet tossed her head. "He looks pretty mature to *me*." She thrust the candy bar into her mouth and snapped off a corner with a savage bite. "Mmm . . . whatever would we do without candy bars?"

Jessica nibbled her lower lip. She wished Janet would shut up about Eric. About the only thing worse than losing Eric to her sister would be losing Eric to Janet. "But—what about Denny?" she ventured. Denny Jacobson was Janet's sort-of boyfriend. "How can you be interested in Eric when—"

Janet made her mouth a tight line. *"Denny?"* she asked, raising one eyebrow. "You mean Denny Jacobson, who's been flirting with Sally Walker ever since we got here?" Sally Walker was a very pretty but fairly shy sixth-grader. Janet went on, "You mean Denny Make-a-fool-of-myself Jacobson, who thinks he's so incredibly cute he can get a dorky little sixth-grader interested in him? If he had any idea how ridiculous he looks with a *kid* like Sally . . ." Her voice trailed off, and she stared malevolently out at the dance floor.

Just as ridiculous as you'd look with Eric, Jessica thought with a sigh, but of course she didn't say so.

*   *   *

"Hi, Eric," Elizabeth said shyly. She could feel her cheeks turn pink, the way they always did when she was talking to a cute guy. "I'm glad you could make it."

"Me too," Eric said. "Where's the eats? I'm starving." He smiled at Elizabeth. "Sorry, I can't remember which one you are."

Elizabeth smiled back. "A lot of people have that problem," she said. "I'm Elizabeth. You can tell by my pendant." She held the agate away from her green sweater. "See?"

"Oh, right!" A huge grin spread across Eric's face. "The agate. Sure, how could I forget?"

Elizabeth let out a whoosh of air. He remembered, then. She'd kind of known he would, but it was nice to be sure. "The snacks are this way," she said, resting her hand loosely on his elbow and steering him toward the tables.

"Cool!" Eric said. "Hey, I'm really glad I ran into you. I wanted to talk to you about sedimentary rocks. I have a ton of them in my collection, and I was wondering if you knew—"

"Eric." A shadow fell in front of Elizabeth. There stood Janet Howell, Jessica's friend. Little warning bells went off inside Elizabeth's head. Janet was definitely *not* one of Elizabeth's all-time favorite people.

"Hi, Janet," Elizabeth said suspiciously, wondering what Janet was up to. She tried to walk around the older girl. "Excuse us, please. We're trying to—"

Janet flashed Eric a brilliant smile. "You must be Eric," she said in a silky voice. "I'm Janet."

Eric blinked. "Nice to know you," he said.

"I've heard *so* much about you," Janet purred. Gently she reached for Eric's elbow.

Elizabeth swallowed hard. "Isn't that Lila over there, Janet?" she lied. "I think she's calling you—"

"Oh, I think Lila can wait," Janet said, steel in her voice. With a quick movement she stepped between Eric and Elizabeth. "I just want to get to know you a little better, Eric," she added softly.

"Um, Janet—" Elizabeth said helplessly. She tried to sidle around Janet but couldn't quite squeeze past. "If you don't *mind*, Eric and I were having a conversation—"

"Later," Janet snapped. "You're incredibly cute; did anybody ever tell you that?"

Eric turned red. "Um—" he began.

"Just as I thought," Janet said smoothly. Taking Eric by the shoulder, she guided him around Elizabeth and onto the dance floor. "See you later, Elizabeth," she said mockingly.

"Um, later," Eric mumbled as Janet swept him away.

Later. Elizabeth squeezed her eyes shut tight. *Darn, darn, darn,* she thought bleakly. *Darn that old Janet.*

And just when things had been going so well too.

*   *   *

Jessica watched, annoyed, as Janet whirled around the dance floor with Eric. *What a rat*, she thought grimly, and she didn't mean Eric. She leaned against the snack table and shook her head sadly. *Some friend Janet is.*

"So how's your rock collection coming along, Elizabeth?" Amy Sutton asked.

Jessica whirled around. Amy, one of Elizabeth's best friends, was pouring herself a glass of lemonade. Maria Slater, another of her sister's best buddies, was nearby, and Elizabeth was across the table looking bummed and munching on a pretzel. *Great*, she thought, her shoulders sagging. *I get to listen to even more rock collection talk.*

But it was too much trouble to leave.

"Pretty good," Elizabeth answered. "I got three new specimens on Thursday." She looked quickly toward the dance floor, frowned briefly, and grinned at Amy. "I have an especially nice piece of quartzite."

"Is that the rock that peels?" Maria asked.

Elizabeth laughed. "No, that's mica. Quartzite is mostly white, and it sparkles."

Jessica exhaled slowly. She could feel blood throbbing in her temples, the way it always did when someone was discussing something boring. Probably it was a medical condition, and she should get to be excused from boring classes like social studies and science because she had it. All the same, she couldn't help feeling a little jealous of her sister. Elizabeth's friends seemed genuinely interested in her hobbies. Jessica's friend, on the other hand, took away her boyfriend.

Well, OK, so he wasn't exactly her boyfriend yet, but she was working on it.

"How are you, Jessica?" Maria asked, noticing her for the first time. "Enjoying the party?"

"I guess," Jessica grumbled. She shaded her eyes against the bright lights and stared out onto the dance floor. The music was ending. Janet leaned down and said something to Eric, who nodded and smiled.

That should have been me, Jessica thought.

But it wasn't.

Jessica pursed her lips. And there was only one reason why it wasn't.

A reason whose name she wouldn't say, but whose initials were Janet Howell. . . .

"Well, a diamond is just a piece of coal that's been under pressure," Elizabeth explained. She grinned at her audience—Maria and Amy—and even Jessica, who seemed to be listening a little. Getting a chance to discuss rocks with her friends almost made up for what Janet had done.

Almost. But not quite.

"Cool," Maria commented, running her fingers through her styled dark hair. "So I could go out and buy a ton of coal and put it under pressure for a while and it would turn to diamonds? I could be rich!"

Elizabeth shook her head. "Only if you had a couple million years to spare."

"Oh, great." A voice groaned. "She's talking about rocks and minerals again. Jessica, will you please shut your sister up?"

Elizabeth started. Janet was standing in front of her, a sneer on her face, and Lila Fowler was at Janet's side. Elizabeth blinked, searching for Eric. "Where's Eric?" she asked hopefully.

"The little boys' room," Janet proclaimed. "He'll be back." She elbowed Jessica in the ribs. "So does your sister ever talk about anything except rocks?"

"You know what they say." Lila snickered. "Rocks on the brain, rocks in the head."

"Real funny," Amy commented.

"No autographs, please," Lila said, blinking furiously and sweeping into a low bow.

Sheesh. Elizabeth tried her best to ignore Janet and Lila. "Anyway, about those diamonds," she began again.

Janet's eyes flashed. Behind her Elizabeth could see Denny Jacobson dancing with Sally Walker, her hands resting loosely on his. "Like I *said*, Jessica," she remarked, arching her eyebrows.

"Yeah," Lila added. "Like she *said*. Um—what was it you said, Janet?"

Janet folded her arms and fixed Elizabeth with a stare. "I *said*," she repeated in a low voice, "there are plenty of *interesting* things a person could do with her free time. And that doesn't include rock collecting."

"Right," Lila said airily. "Jessica, tell your sister to cut out collecting rocks right now. It's bad for the image of the Unicorn Club."

"What does Elizabeth's collection have to do with the Unicorns?" Maria wanted to know. "She's not even a member of your silly club."

Janet popped a chocolate drop into her mouth. "It's true that we don't usually consider a person's sister's hobbies when we invite them to join the Unicorns," she said, chewing. "But I've been thinking we ought to make a new policy about that."

Elizabeth scuffed her toe angrily on the floor of the ballroom. *Here it comes*, she thought. She knew Jessica well enough to know that her twin was a totally different person when she was with the Unicorns. *She'll say something mean*, she predicted, *just to show she belongs with Janet and Lila . . . and I'll probably say something mean back because we've gotten into the habit of arguing a lot lately . . . and before you know it, we'll be in a huge fight. . . .*

She swallowed hard. *And then Mom will find out, and we'll have broken our New Year's resolution before we even started, practically, and Steven will get to go skiing, and we'll be stuck at home with each other.*

Elizabeth squeezed her eyes shut tight. What a stupid party. What a stupid world.

And it was all Janet's fault.

*   *   *

"Tell her off, Jessica," Janet ordered, grabbing three more chocolate drops.

Jessica took a deep breath and looked down at the floor. She knew she'd need plenty of courage for what she was about to do. "Well, actually, Janet," she said in a strangled voice, "I don't think you ought to be picking on my sister like that."

Elizabeth's eyes flew open. "Huh?" she asked, blinking hard.

"I beg your pardon?" Janet asked in an icy voice.

Jessica's mouth felt dry. She swallowed hard, then swallowed again, harder. Standing up to Janet was incredibly difficult, but she didn't really have a choice. *If I start going after Elizabeth*, she told herself, *Lizzie'll scream at me, and we'll be in an argument before you can say "spring break," and poof, there goes our resolution. And Steven will go skiing without us, and he'll never quit teasing me about it till the day he dies. . . .* She stared harder at the floor, half hoping it would open and swallow her up. "I mean," she went on, her determination growing, "Elizabeth can collect what she wants. Not that *I'd* want to collect rocks or anything," she added quickly. "But if Elizabeth wants to, it's OK with me."

There was silence. Jessica held her breath and raised her eyes just a bit. In the distance she could see Denny and Sally dancing together. *Well, I've done it*, she thought, feeling numb.

A grin spread across Elizabeth's face. "Um,

thanks," she said shyly. Her eyes met her twin's and held her gaze for a second before Jessica looked back to the floor.

"Whoa!" Maria raised her eyebrows. "This can't be Jessica Wakefield, can it?"

"OK, Jessica, admit it. Aliens have taken over your body, right?" Janet said, narrowing her eyes.

"N-No." Jessica shook her head, slowly at first, then faster. She moistened her lips. "It's—it's just that . . ." Her voice trailed off, and she looked to Elizabeth for help.

"It's our New Year's resolution," Elizabeth supplied. Jessica gave a slight nod. "We've resolved not to fight for a whole week."

"A whole week! Sounds hard," Maria observed, smiling broadly. "No, seriously, guys, good luck to you both."

"Thanks," Jessica said, still not daring to look at Janet. Her heart was beating furiously.

"It's not going to be easy," Elizabeth said. "But I think we can do it."

Jessica rolled her eyes. Was that some kind of a slam? "I *know* we can do it," she said with more confidence than she felt.

Elizabeth shrugged. "Think, know, same difference," she said in a brittle voice.

Yeah, right, Jessica thought. Still, she didn't want to get annoyed at her sister. "Whatever," she said brightly. "Do you guys have any resolutions of your own? Since it's New Year's Eve and all?"

"I'll stop fighting with *my* sister," Lila said.

Maria made a harrumphing noise. "No problem, Lila, seeing as you don't have one. Actually I probably should make a resolution. I just don't know what."

Janet glanced over her shoulder. "I could think of a million things," she said casually. "For you, I mean. As for me, well—that's a different story."

Jessica let out a breath. "You're so right, Janet," she said, moving closer to her friend. If Janet was picking on somebody besides her, maybe things would be OK.

"Dream on," Amy said sarcastically. "OK. As a show of support for the Wakefield twins, I'm going to make a resolution too. For a week anyway. Let's see. . . ." She stared at the ceiling. "Got it! I love to sleep in, but I've been late to school *way* too many times this year. I hereby resolve not to be tardy next week."

"Good luck with *that* one," Elizabeth told her friend.

Maria stroked her cheeks. "And I hereby resolve not to look in any mirrors," she said slowly. "To admire myself, I mean. Bad Hollywood habit."

Jessica managed a weak grin. Maria had been a child movie star before moving to Sweet Valley.

Lila sniffed. "Resolutions are for *kids*. Right, Janet?"

Janet waved her hand in the air. "Resolutions are no big deal."

"That's what I meant," Lila added quickly.

Janet scowled. "If you decide to do something, you do it. Simple as that. Only weak people make resolutions. I never have any trouble doing anything once I've made up my mind to do it." She tapped her forehead significantly and then grabbed another handful of chocolate drops.

"Prove it," Amy said.

"Excuse me?" Janet paused with the first drop halfway to her mouth.

"Prove it," Amy repeated. She gestured to Jessica. "Jessica's making a resolution. So am I. So are Elizabeth and Maria. I wonder if you could keep one too." Folding her arms, she nodded at the candy in Janet's hand. "I've noticed you have a real sweet tooth. Give up candy. I bet you can't!"

"Of course I can," Janet boasted. She dropped the drops back into the bowl on the table. "Who are you to say I can't do whatever I put my mind to? It's against my principles, but OK. I hereby resolve to give up sweets for one whole week. It'll be easy."

Jessica gave a crooked grin. "How about you, Lila?" she asked. "Let's make a game out of it. We'll all make resolutions, and the last one to give in wins a prize."

Lila made a face. "Forget prizes," she said. "Penalties are better. Like, whoever doesn't make it has to do something really disgusting. Something like—" She hesitated. "Like wearing a diaper."

Elizabeth raised her eyebrows. "What do you mean?"

"We'll do it like this," Janet said before Lila could speak. "We all have resolutions, right? Well, in a week I'll have a party at my house." She glanced around the circle. "I suppose I'll have to invite you three." She sighed, indicating Amy, Maria, and Elizabeth.

"Get to the point," Amy said impatiently.

"Anybody who's broken their resolution," Janet said, a gleam in her eye, "will have to wear a baby diaper all night long. No exceptions. Agreed?"

"Um—" Jessica wiped her forehead. It would be another reason to avoid fighting with Elizabeth, that was for sure. And it would be kind of fun to see who showed up in a diaper. She caught her sister's eye.

"A . . . diaper?" Elizabeth's voice trailed off.

"Not a disposable diaper," Janet snapped. "No, I mean cloth ones. They come in pretty big sizes. The losers will have to safety pin them over their pants," she added.

"Oh," Elizabeth murmured, relieved. "I knew that."

"And nobody tells anybody who isn't in the game what's going on. I don't want a bunch of loser kids begging to get in the game and then showing up at *my* house at *my* party. Agreed?" Janet's eyes glittered.

"Agreed," Jessica said hastily. Better to be back on Janet's good side. "Great idea, Janet," she said in her heartiest voice and clapped Janet on the back.

"Even better," Janet pronounced, "I'll get my

brother, Joe, to come too, maybe bring some of his friends. Like your brother," she said to Jessica. "And they'll have to make resolutions too."

Amy's eyes widened. "Cool!"

"Yeah," Elizabeth agreed. "It *would* be fun to see Steven in a diaper." Her eyes danced mischievously. "Sure. Count me in. *If* Lila makes a resolution too."

"Me?" Lila put her hand to her chest. "Surely you jest. I'm perfect already."

Amy stifled a snicker. "Your worst fault is bragging. So I'll make your resolution for you. Repeat after me: 'I, Lila Fowler.'"

Lila made a face.

"Say it," Janet hissed, stepping sharply on her friend's foot.

"'I, Lila Fowler,'" Lila said in a bored tone of voice.

"'Do hereby resolve,'" Amy went on.

"'Do hereby resolve.'" Lila yawned.

"'Not to brag for a whole week,'" Amy finished.

"'Not to brag for a whole week,'" Lila said. "Oooh, that'll be so hard," she added sarcastically.

"Oh, here comes someone interesting," Janet remarked. "Catch you later—in *diapers*." Turning quickly, she headed for the dance floor and waved frantically to Eric.

Jessica grimaced. It would be fun to see if everybody could keep up their resolutions. But there was one person she really, *really* wanted to see fail.

Her so-called Majesty, Janet Howell.

Five

It was Sunday afternoon, the day before vacation would be officially over. Steven made a face and leaned wearily against the windowsill. Rain streaked the pane. Thunder rolled in the distance. *The perfect day for watching TV,* Steven told himself with a scowl. *Like, what else is there to do?*

He looked longingly at the dark and silent screen in the corner of the living room. For crying out loud, he was missing some of his favorite shows. *Fine French Cooking with Fred. True Alien Abductions!* And that adventure series about the family trying to find their way out of the old abandoned coal mine . . . what was that one called anyway? His fingers itched for the remote.

The trouble with making a resolution was that people expected you to keep it. Especially when you were stupid enough to promise to cancel yourself out of a ski trip if you broke it. *Dumb, dumb, dumb.* Steven tapped his knuckles against his head and stared out at the rain. And the worst was that he'd even agreed to that so-called game about breaking New Year's resolutions. That stupid game where you had to wear a diaper if you broke the resolution. If he'd thought about it, he'd have chosen something besides watching TV. Something easier to manage. Like maybe, "I resolve not to try out for the Lakers this year." Or, "I resolve to be one of the five or six best-looking guys at Sweet Valley High School." Something like that.

He breathed hard on the windowpane and watched the window mist up. Speaking of resolutions, the twins had been getting along awfully well for the last couple of days. More like they usually did. It was beginning to weird him out. Idly he traced the initials EW on the top half and the initials JW on the bottom. Elizabeth and Jessica. He wished they'd blow it. Then they'd have to wear diapers. And they'd have to skip the ski trip. With a quick stroke of his wrist he wiped his sleeve against the initials. If only it was so easy to just wipe away their resolution—

Wait a minute.

Steven sat still. Who said the twins had to fight all by themselves? Who said they couldn't have a little help? He'd tried to do that once already, just after the twins made their resolution. But he hadn't tried hard. Not like he *could* try if he really *wanted* to.

Slowly he got to his feet. *Cupcakes*, he thought. *Cupcakes.* There had been two gooey cupcakes in the box last time he'd looked. What would happen if the twins went to the pantry for dessert and found only one cupcake—for the two of them?

The fur would fly, that was what. And then they could say *sayonara* to the ski trip. *Yes, indeedy.*

Whistling happily, Steven headed for the kitchen.

"Like the blouse?" Elizabeth asked, a dreamy look in her eyes. She stood outside Casey's, admiring herself in the reflection off the window glass. "I saw it in the boutique, and I just had to have it."

Jessica gulped. The blouse was the dweebiest thing she had ever seen in her entire life. Green and yellow with large brown buttons, it looked like something a pioneer woman would have worn. If her other three shirts were all in the wash.

"Don't you like it?" Elizabeth glanced over her shoulder, a frown on her face. "It was even on sale—less than twenty dollars! Can you believe it?"

Jessica took a deep breath. Oh, she could believe it was less than twenty dollars, all right. She could believe it was less than *five* dollars. She could believe the store actually *paid* people to take that style off their hands. Jessica opened her mouth to tell her sister exactly what she thought of her new blouse—and then she hesitated.

"You don't like it—do you?" Elizabeth's lower lip drooped.

Jessica moistened her lips. If she told the truth, what would happen next? She'd hurt her sister's feelings for no good reason, and then Elizabeth would feel like she had to say something mean back, and the next thing you knew, they'd be having a big fight. . . . She swallowed her words and pasted a huge smile on her face.

"What gives you *that* idea? I love it!" she gushed, crossing her fingers nimbly behind her back. "I think it goes so well with your . . . um, nose. Yeah, your nose. And your eyebrows too," she added quickly.

Elizabeth smiled back. "Oh, I'm *so* glad you like it," she said with feeling. "For some strange reason, I don't know why, I kind of thought maybe you wouldn't!"

Phew. Jessica heaved a sigh of relief. She'd dodged that bullet.

But this resolution was taking an awful lot out of her, that was for sure.

She wasn't sure how much longer she could keep it up.

"Hey, guys! What are you doing here?"

Jessica waved frantically across the mall concourse. Elizabeth groaned under her breath. Coming up the escalator were Ellen Riteman, Kimberly Haver, and Grace Oliver. Three Unicorns.

Ellen got off the escalator, her blue eyes sparkling in the light. "Hi, Jessica! Hi, Elizabeth."

"This is *so* cool, running into you like this," Jessica said enthusiastically. "What are you doing here anyway?"

Kimberly patted her wavy brown hair and rested her elbow on Grace's shoulder. Elizabeth couldn't help a grin; Kimberly was a tall seventh-grader and Grace was one of the shortest girls in the entire sixth grade. "Hitting the movies. Kind of a last minute good-bye to vacation."

"Yeah," Grace said gloomily. "School tomorrow, yuck."

Elizabeth was about to say that she was looking forward to school starting up again, but she decided she'd better not. Instead she scowled and sighed with Jessica. "Yeah, what a bummer," she said.

"What movie are you going to see?" Jessica asked.

"The latest Arnold Weissenhammer flick," Ellen answered. "You know, *Desert Tornado*? When he's in the Sahara, escaping from terrorists and stuff?"

"Cool!" Jessica's eyes lit up. "I haven't seen that one yet. Maybe we should go too. What do you say, Elizabeth?"

What do I say? Elizabeth gulped. "Su-Sure," she stammered, smiling brightly and crossing her fingers behind her back. "It'd be, you know, fun to spend some time with you guys."

It was possibly the biggest lie she'd ever told in her life. Ellen, Kimberly, and Grace were pretty shallow people, even for Unicorns. And as for the Arnold Weissenhammer movie, well, the less said about *that* the better.

But if she said no, then Jessica might get mad. And then Elizabeth would have a hard time not snapping back. And before you knew it, there'd be a big argument. And she'd be out a ski trip. And she'd have to show up at Janet's house in a diaper.

All the same, it would have been much easier if Jessica's friends had—well, better taste.

"I'm sure the movie's going to be really cool," she lied, beaming at Kimberly.

"Well, I don't know, Lila," Janet Howell was saying into the telephone. "You see, I have much more *strength* than any of the rest of them do." She listened for a moment. "For me willpower is easy. A snap. Don't you understand *anything?*"

Joe pretended to gag. He lay stretched out in the living room, a paperback open in front of him, but he was really listening to his sister's conversation. Janet always sounded so . . . so *perfect.* Not perfect perfect: nauseatingly perfect. Like that woman on TV who was always grinning while she told her audience how they could make planters out of used paper cups and turn their empty toilet paper rolls into kicky little napkin holders. What was her name? He'd have to check with Wakefield.

"What are you talking about?" Janet's hand flew to her chest. "*Moi?* I haven't even *looked* at a piece of chocolate since New Year's Eve."

A smile played around Joe's lips. *Right, the resolution,* he thought. Actually he had to hand it to his sister. Janet really had been staying away from candy lately. Last week she'd polished off a whole bag of chocolate drops in less than two days. But since New Year's she hadn't touched a single one of the caramels, lemon creams, or toffees in the box tucked at the bottom of the pantry. Joe knew because he counted them every day. He was desperate to see his swelled-head little sister in a diaper.

Joe leaned closer, hoping to hear what Janet would say next.

"Well, I'd better go, Li," Janet said, giving her brother a look. "A certain person doesn't remember about the right to *privacy*." She slammed down the phone. "I guess you want to use the phone, Joe," she said sarcastically.

"Um—" Joe swallowed hard and nodded. "Um, yeah. I guess. If it's not, like, too much trouble. If you're done and everything."

Janet smiled. "In case you didn't hear, big brother, *I* have been sticking to my resolution like glue. How about you?" She snickered. "Glue, you. It rhymes. Get it?"

"Real cute, Janet," Joe said. "For your information, I've been doing just fine on my resolution. So why don't *you* grab a *clue*? Get it?" He grinned, showing his teeth. "I haven't been to Casey's in two whole days, OK? So get off my back."

"Like it's so *hard* to stay away from Casey's. . . ." Janet grunted. Batting her eyelashes at her brother mockingly, she strode from the room.

She's gone, Joe told himself, biting his lip. He

hunched closer to the phone and pressed "talk." The dial tone hummed in his ear. *Well, here goes nothing.*

Slowly he pulled a scrap of paper out of his pocket and stared at the seven numbers scrawled on it. His heart hammered. If he waited long enough, maybe he wouldn't have to make the call. Maybe the roof would cave in or the phone company would cancel their service or something. . . .

But in his heart of hearts he knew that wasn't going to happen.

Not going to Casey's was Joe's public resolution. If he blew it, he'd have to wear a stupid diaper to the party. *Big deal.* Joe was fairly sure he could make it for a week without Casey's, though those Super Sundaes were awfully tempting when he knew he couldn't have one.

But secretly Joe had made a private resolution too. A resolution that no one knew about but him. A resolution to invite a certain person out. Preferably to the party that would be at his house next Friday.

A resolution to call up Patty. Patty Weinberg.

He shut his short-story book and poised his forefinger over the phone. *Do it,* he commanded himself silently.

But what if she says no or laughs in your ear or something? a voice whispered in his head.

Gritting his teeth, Joe pressed the first digit, then the second, and then the third. Then he paused for breath—

And heard a key jingling in the lock.

"I'm home!" his mother's voice called. "Joe,

Janet, please come help with the groceries!"

"Darn," Joe said aloud, but inwardly he was smiling. Quickly he hung up the phone. This was obviously no time to be making phone calls. "Coming, Mom!" he called out, jumping up and heading for the door.

He'd just have to call Patty some other time, that was all.

No big deal.

"So Mr. and Mrs. Howell asked us to help chaperone your party next Friday," Mr. Wakefield said, pushing away his dinner plate with a sigh.

Elizabeth looked interested. "And are you going to?" She laid her fork on the table and set her napkin neatly beside it.

"We said yes," Mr. Wakefield said. "The things we do for our children. . . ."

Steven rolled his eyes. "You're afraid of a bunch of teenagers, Dad? And teenager wannabes?" he added quickly just in case anybody got the idea that his sisters were teenagers yet. Which they weren't. "You'll probably die of boredom watching us dance and scarf down chips and salsa." He wolfed down the last scraps of mashed potatoes on his plate and checked the bowl for more, but it was empty.

Mr. Wakefield smiled. "Who says we'll just be watching and not dancing? And your mother and I love chips and salsa."

Steven rolled his eyes. *As if hanging out with my sis-*

ters won't be embarrassing enough. "Speaking of chips
and salsa . . . ," he began, peeking at his sisters. "How
about, um, dessert?" He made smacking noises with
his lips. *That ought to get them going.* "Dessert," Jessica
said slowly. "There's only one thing I can think of that
would still go in my stomach right now," she said. "A
cupcake. A nice, big, thick, gooey chocolate cupcake."

"Me too," Elizabeth said. "A cupcake sounds
perfect. I think there are two left. Who wants one?"

Mrs. Wakefield shook her head. Mr. Wakefield
held up his hand. "No, thanks," they said in unison.

"Not I," Steven said in the most bored voice he
could muster. He'd counted on his parents turning
down the cupcakes: They usually only went for
cupcakes from a real live bakery, not the kind you
got in the box at the supermarket. "I shall allow my
siblings to each have one of her own."

"Well, that's very nice of you, Steven!" Mrs.
Wakefield said, smiling.

Steven watched through heavily lidded eyes as his
sisters stood up. *Hee, hee,* he thought. Visions of what
was to come floated through his mind: Elizabeth saying, "But I want it," Jessica saying, "But I said it first,"
Elizabeth getting all huffy and saying, "That doesn't
mean anything," Jessica saying, "Well, who died and
made you queen of the universe?" and then Mom
and Dad saying, "Forget that trip, you two!" *Yup.* He
sat up straight, trying not to smile too much.

"Poor Janet," Jessica said as she left the room.

"No sweets for a *week*. I feel *so* sorry for her."

And poor Joe, Steven thought. *No Casey's for a week.* He hadn't decided whether to be a real pal and stay away from Casey's himself—as much as was *reasonable* anyway—or whether to drive his buddy totally insane and go to Casey's three times a day.

"Uh-oh," Elizabeth said from the kitchen. "What happened to the other one?"

Here it comes. Steven clasped his hands together in anticipation.

"Someone must have eaten it," Jessica replied in an annoyed tone. "Well, that's OK. I thought about this one first, so I'll—"

"Wait just a minute," Elizabeth said warningly. "Who said you—"

There was a pause.

"Hear that, Mom?" Steven gestured offhandedly to the kitchen. Inside, his heart was singing. *Diapers, here we come!* he thought gleefully. "Gee, sounds like the twins are having an argument or something."

Mrs. Wakefield flashed an irritated look at her husband. "After all we've been through about this. Ned, would you go talk to them, please?"

Mr. Wakefield sighed and shoved back his chair. But before he could stand up, the girls were back in the dining room, each holding half a cupcake in her hand.

Steven blinked. "What's . . . going on?" he asked, frowning.

"Nothing," Jessica said airily. "There was only

one cupcake left, so we split it."

"That was very mature of you," Mrs. Wakefield said approvingly. "I'm proud of you both."

Darn. Steven rolled his eyes. "I think Elizabeth has a little more frosting than you do," he said, leaning across the table to Jessica.

Jessica gave him a cool stare. "Maybe," she said casually. "But that's OK. I probably have a little more cake than she does."

"It doesn't really matter anyway," Elizabeth added in a bored voice. "When you're mature and responsible, you can't be bothered with silly details like the amount of frosting."

"Good for you," Mr. Wakefield said heartily. "At this rate you'll be able to manage the ski trip after all."

"I'm sure we will," Elizabeth said, biting into her half of the cupcake.

"Me too," Jessica agreed, her mouth full.

Steven wrinkled his nose and stared down at his plate.

What was it that Ratshark always said when he was arrested at the end of every episode and brought to the Ratjail? *Rats! Sharked again!* That was it. That was how he felt just now. Totally sharked.

But there was plenty of time left. He nodded slowly. *Yeah.*

He'd get them.

Six

◇

"OK, guys, here's a scorecard for the resolution game," Maria said at lunch the next day. She handed a sheet of paper to Elizabeth and another just like it to Amy. "I used my parents' spreadsheet program on the computer. Everybody gets one. Cool, isn't it?"

Elizabeth peered at the paper. It *was* cool, she had to admit. There were three columns. The first was labeled Name, the second Resolution, and the third Kill.

"I'll bring a copy home for Steven," she promised, tapping her finger on the third column. "Kill? What's this mean?"

Maria grinned. "Nothing much," she said in a casual tone of voice. "If somebody breaks their resolution, we put a big X in the box, that's all. It's like they're dead or something."

"But why 'kill'?" Elizabeth wanted to know.

Maria fidgeted in her seat. "It was, um, Amy's idea," she admitted. "Why don't you tell her, Amy?"

Amy burst into a grin. "I was just thinking. I'd like to be supportive of most of these resolutions. Like Maria's and yours. But there are a couple of other people who I thought—" She hesitated and took a bite of brownie. "Well, there's a certain person I *don't* want to be supportive of at all," she said, chewing. "There's a certain person I'm going to try to get out of the game just as soon as possible." Her eyes gleamed.

"A certain person who is rude, obnoxious, self-centered, and a lot of other things, but I ran out of adjectives," Maria went on.

Elizabeth shifted in her seat and took a quick look at the Unicorner, the table where the Unicorns usually sat. A certain person was sitting at the head of the table, gesturing broadly, her mouth going a mile a minute while the other girls all listened. "Janet?" she whispered.

"Got it in one," Maria said, smiling.

Amy made a gun out of her forefinger and thumb and pointed it at Janet. *"Zap!"* she said, pretending to pull the trigger. Her face turned pink. "I guess it's not very nice, Elizabeth . . . but I did want to get Janet. And it just felt like if we called it a kill, it would seem somehow more—more—"

"More dangerous," Maria put in. She stood up

and grabbed a handful of scorecards. "Wish me luck," she said dryly. "I'm going to invade the Unicorner to pass these out."

Elizabeth couldn't help smiling. "A kill," she mused aloud, taking a sip of milk as Maria left. "Sounds good to me." She hastily scanned the list of players in the resolution game. Jessica, Maria, Lila, Janet, Amy, herself, Steven, Joe . . .

A kill. Yeah. She nodded, remembering how obnoxious Janet had been at the party. *"Only weak people make resolutions." That's what Janet said.*

If there was one player on that list she'd like to kill, it would be Janet Howell.

Dinner was over, and Steven was sitting up in his room busily not doing his homework. Instead his eyes flicked rapidly down the scorecard the twins had given him. It was kind of fun to see what everyone had chosen. *Lila—no bragging.* That one would last about five seconds, he told himself with a smirk. *Jessica—no arguing. Steven—no TV. Janet—*

"*Ratshark!*" a voice boomed down in the living room. "*Yes, it's Ratshark, the villain you love to hate!*"

Ratshark. Steven got unsteadily to his feet. The twins must be watching TV downstairs, he decided. He wondered which episode this was. Probably a good one. He'd always thought *Ratshark* was one of the better shows on TV these days. Opening the door to his room, he stood in the upstairs hallway, humming along as the *Ratshark* theme song played.

"What a great show," Jessica said loudly.

"It sure is," Elizabeth agreed over the music.

"'His bite is worse than his bark,'" Steven sang. "'You'll see him whenever it's dark.'" In his mind's eye he could see the star of the cartoon, the little half rat, half shark with the humongous teeth, swimming along near the Ratjail as the opening credits rolled. "'Beware of him at night in the park; he's'"—*rest, rest*—"'Rat-*shark!*'"

Cautiously Steven crept down the first three stairs.

"Too bad *Steven* can't watch," Jessica said in an even louder voice.

"Really," Elizabeth shouted. "Such a shame. I think this is a new episode!"

A new episode. Steven's pulse quickened. He went down two more steps. They always caught Ratshark at the end and put him in prison, but it was interesting to see how they caught him on each show. Steven also liked to see what crime Ratshark was planning to commit in every episode. By leaning forward, he could see through the rails on the banister and into the living room. If he moved just a little to the right, he could sort of faintly make out the TV screen, which had gone to a commercial. It was kind of an awkward position, but—

"But I guess Steven is upstairs doing his

homework, like a good boy," Jessica remarked at the top of her lungs.

"I sure hope so," Elizabeth added. "Otherwise he'd be out of the game." She drew a big *X* in the air. "And we'd get credit for a kill."

"Yup," Jessica said. Abruptly she turned toward the stairs. Steven froze, but it was too late. Jessica's lips curled into a big grin. "Speaking of brothers, Lizzie, look at that!"

"Oh, my," Elizabeth said, swiveling around. "Hi, Steven. Not breaking your New Year's resolution already, are you?"

"Do we have a confirmed kill here?" Jessica grinned broadly.

"Who, me?" Steven squawked. He stood up straight. "Oh, no," he lied, massaging a crick in his neck and coming down the staircase so he could see his sisters. "I wasn't watching TV at all," he said, his heart pounding. "You can't even *see* the TV set from up there, ha, ha."

"Then what were you doing all bent over like that?" Jessica stuck out her lower lip and stared meaningfully at her brother.

Talk fast, Wakefield! "Um—I dropped my pencil," Steven fibbed, flashing the twins his biggest grin. "You know how pencils are. It just, like, dropped. Then it started, you know, rolling down the steps, boom, boom, boom?" He demonstrated with his hand. "When it stopped, I had to reach for it, and it was way to the side almost under the carpet. What a bummer." He laughed easily, hoping his sisters would buy it.

Jessica sighed. "The pencil fell off your desk?"

"Kind of a long way to roll, isn't it?" Elizabeth chimed in.

"Off my *desk?*" Steven stifled a snort. He waved his hand in the air as if to ask what planet his sisters were from. Then he dug his hand into his pocket, hoping against hope that he'd find what he was looking for. "Surely you jest. No, no, I was on my way downstairs to have, um, a snack when my pencil so *rudely* slipped out of my tight little grasp and—" *Ha!* Proof positive. A pencil stub was tucked away in his right pants pocket, left over from chemistry class this morning. He held it aloft proudly. "See?"

"Spare me, Steven." Jessica grunted. "I guess we'll have to let you off the hook. *This* time."

Phew. Steven's heart returned to normal. "That was a close call. *I'll have to be more careful,* Steven thought. *Nobody's going to zap Steven Wakefield!*

Seven

"Mmm-mmm, delicious," Amy said, biting off a huge chunk of chocolate chip cookie. She smacked her lips and chewed. "I'm so glad I have mmf mmf mrfle."

"I beg your pardon?" Elizabeth frowned at her friend.

Amy swallowed. "I'm so glad I have a couple of big chocolate chip cookies in my lunch," she remarked loudly. "I could even give one away to a friend. If I *wanted* to." Her gaze was directed somewhere over Elizabeth's left shoulder.

Elizabeth stared at Amy's cookie. It was big and round and brown, and it looked homemade. Her mouth watered. "Well, if you're really planning to give it away," she said, trying not to sound greedy.

"Not you," Amy hissed. "I'm, um, trying to kill Janet."

Kill Janet . . . For a moment Elizabeth's heart thudded against her chest. Then she remembered the resolution game, and her pulse returned to normal. She glanced over her shoulder. "What do you mean?"

"Janet's right there." Amy chewed deliberately and held what was left of her cookie in the air. "She can see me plain as day. I've got—let's see—a couple more cookies, a piece of cake, a slice of pie, and three chocolate bars." She swallowed again, coughing as she did so. "And I aim to sit here and eat them one after another until Janet notices me and starts begging me for just a tiny bite."

So that was why Amy was sitting so close to the Unicorner today. "And then?" Elizabeth raised her eyebrows.

Amy patted her stomach. "And I'll say, 'One, I guess,' and Janet will bite in like a hungry wolf, and I'll say, *'You're busted!'*" She eyed the rest of her cookie. "Of course, I have to finish all the rest of this stuff. Mom doesn't like it if I waste food. But if I can kill Janet the Obnoxious—" She smiled at Elizabeth.

"Then a little stomachache will be worth it!"

"Mmm-mmm, delicious," Lila said, licking her fork daintily. "Gee, guys, you really should get some of this luscious double-fudge chocolate layer cake before it's all gone!"

Jessica eyed Lila's plate hungrily. She'd already had a piece of her own, but the two slices Lila had brought back seemed even more wonderful than the one she'd eaten. "It looks good," she said, leaning over.

Lila waved Jessica's hand away. "You've already had yours. It's Janet I'm worrying about," she continued sorrowfully, not quite looking in her direction. "I know how much she loves sweets, and this cake, well—" She smacked her lips and took another tiny bite. "I'd hate to think that she's going to miss it altogether."

Jessica glanced across the tablet. Janet's mouth was open, and Jessica thought she could see her friend's tongue along her lips as Lila talked. *Do it, Janet,* she urged in her head. In her mind's eye she could see a big red X drawn by Janet's name on the scorecard. "Yeah, have a bite, Janet," she suggested.

"It's really good." Lila scooped up a bit of frosting and held out the spoon to Janet. *"Really* good."

A tingle of excitement shot up Jessica's spine. "You won't regret it, promise," she said. Her eyes met Lila's. *Janet in diapers* . . . She could hardly wait.

Janet narrowed her eyes. "Thanks, guys, but I don't think so," she said with a light laugh. "I *did* make the resolution, after all."

Jessica's palms felt clammy. "We won't tell," she promised, halfway winking at Lila. *And if you believe that* . . . "Seriously, Janet. We really won't."

"Really," Lila promised.

Janet shrugged. "There's another problem too," she said. "Empty calories. Chocolate makes you gain weight." She leaned innocently forward and stared hard into Lila's eyes. "Aren't you worried about putting on *weight*, Lila?"

"Me?" The spoon quivered in Lila's grasp. "Are you crazy or something? I've never put on an ounce of weight that I didn't personally choose to have." Lila blinked rapidly. "My weight is perfect exactly as it is and—"

Uh-oh. "Cut it out, Lila," Jessica directed her friend.

"And your teeth," Janet said, a sliver of a smile playing around her lips. "Oh, boy, your teeth. Chocolate *kills* your teeth. We're talking megacavities here. How are you planning to—"

"My teeth are *perfect*," Lila interrupted. "No one in this entire cafeteria has teeth that are in as good shape as mine and—" She blinked. "I mean—" Quickly Lila clamped her lips shut tight as she saw Janet grinning at her, but it was too late.

"*Zap!*" Janet stretched out a forefinger at Lila. "First confirmed kill." She smiled mockingly across the table.

"See you in diapers, Lila!"

Joe tossed his books into a pile and stood up from his seat. The bell had just rung, and it was time to leave science class. Another day, another lecture. Not that he really cared all that much about acids and bases and stuff like that. Plus it was hard to concentrate when you were hungry.

He wished he'd brought more lunch. The two hot dogs, three apples, two bags of potato chips, and Hostess Ding Dongs he'd eaten weren't nearly enough for a guy who still hadn't finished his growth spurt, and anyway, lunch had been over an hour ago. Joe swallowed, imagining a frosty, cool, gleaming Super Sundae from Casey's sliding down his throat. . . .

Cut it out! he told himself sternly, picking up his books and heading for the door of the science room. The truth was, he'd been dreaming of Super Sundaes pretty often during the last couple of days. That was no way to keep a resolution. His hand groped in his back pants pocket for the granola bar he carried with him for emergencies, and he walked quickly into the hall—

Wait a minute.

Joe froze. Patty Weinberg was walking in his direction.

And speaking of New Year's resolutions . . .

Joe's heart sped up, and he felt short of breath. He stood still in the middle of the corridor, studying Patty's face. She was *so* good-looking—that upturned nose, the short dark hair, the smile on her face even when she was alone.

Ask her now, you fool, he told himself. *Just step out in front of her and say . . .*

He scratched his head. *And say whatever Wakefield would say,* he finished. *Something like, "Hi, Patty!*

Cool to see you. Hey, I was wondering, do you have any plans or anything for next Friday?" He nodded slowly. "Yeah, that's the ticket, all right," he murmured. He could picture himself standing there suavely, totally at ease, barely noticing while the other kids swirled around them on their way to class, looking deep into Patty's eyes and confidently inviting her out on a date, and she'd be so pleased, she'd give a cry of delight and say, "Sure, Joe. Oh, I've been waiting for you to ask," and . . . and . . .

Joe's head snapped up. He pasted a broad grin on his face. "Patty!" he said in his deepest, most mature voice, stepping into the center of the hall—

Just as Patty, not glancing his way, stepped into the classroom next door to the science lab.

Bummer. Joe licked his lips. He knew he should follow her. But . . . if he did, then he couldn't just say, "Cool to see you," as if he'd just happened to run into her. No. It would be like he was tracking her down. Following her. Which wasn't the same thing at all.

He hefted his books in one hand and rubbed the back of his neck with the other. Funny how he already felt a little more . . . *relaxed* than he had when he'd first seen Patty. Smiling faintly, Joe made up his mind.

He'd wait till tomorrow. Yeah, tomorrow.

With a spring in his step Joe headed off to German class.

*   *   *

"The thing is, I don't feel so great today," Amy said, fingering one of the three doughnuts she'd brought from home. "I don't know why . . . but I did get to school on time at least!" She smiled wanly.

"Hurray!" Elizabeth applauded. It was Wednesday at lunch, and Amy and Elizabeth were sitting with Maria at the table next to the Unicorner.

"This is *so* tasty," Amy declared, biting into the first doughnut. Globs of jelly oozed onto her hand. "*Boy*, I'm glad I brought these today." She licked her hand. "Nothing's better than jelly," she said with a satisfied sigh.

"She isn't paying any attention," Elizabeth said. She stared at Janet, sitting between Lila and Jessica at the next table. If she looked hard, she could see a corner of Janet's scorecard sticking out from her notebook, with a brilliant red X under Kill, by Lila's name. "She's tough, guys."

"I know," Maria suggested. "I'll offer her one. See if she can resist my charms."

Amy pushed one doughnut across the table to Maria. "Thanks," she said, hiccuping. "And if she doesn't take it, eat it yourself, OK?"

"Hey, Janet!" Maria stood up, her hand outstretched. "Amy had an extra doughnut, and she wondered if you'd like it. No strings attached."

Janet smiled. "Thanks," she said, nodding to Amy. "But no thanks. Not today."

"Oh." Maria put on her best actress's pout. "But we thought that of all the people we knew, you'd be the one to appreciate it the most. . . ." Her voice trailed off.

Elizabeth winked at Amy. Just as she'd often thought. Maria would make a great saleswoman.

"I really don't think so, Maria," Janet said, resting her elbow on the table. "Oh—wait a minute—" Frowning, she peered at Maria's face. "What's—that?"

Maria's hand flew to her cheek. "What's what?"

"Oh . . . that zit or whatever it is. . . ." Janet stroked her own cheek absentmindedly. "Probably nothing to worry about or anything. Still, better to be sure . . ." She reached for her handbag.

Elizabeth narrowed her eyes. If there was anything wrong with Maria's face, *she* certainly couldn't see it.

"Sometimes jelly will make you break out," Janet said sadly. "Acne and all. Here, take a look." She produced a small hand mirror and gave it to Maria. "You know, too many doughnuts. . . . It *does* look like a zit, but I guess it could be a mole. Maybe you ought to see a doctor."

"A doctor?" Maria's eyes bulged as she held the mirror to her face.

Elizabeth stirred uneasily in her seat, watching her friend. Something was wrong here, but she couldn't quite put her finger on what. Her eyes shifted from Maria to Janet and back.

"I don't see anything." Maria sounded confused.

She turned the mirror this way and that. "There's, like, a tiny beauty mark over here, as usual, but my skin is as smooth as it's always been."

Janet's lips curved into a mocking smile.

"Put it down!" Elizabeth cried, suddenly realizing what Janet was up to, but it was too late. Janet's forefinger had already zoomed out.

"Zap!" she shouted. "Admiring yourself in a mirror breaks your New Year's resolution!" She pulled her scorecard out of her notebook and drew a big red X next to Maria's name. Then she raised her arms over her head like a heavyweight boxer who'd just knocked out an opponent.

"Two confirmed kills for Janet!"

Eight

◇

"How about a milk shake?" Amy asked. She stared up at the Dairi Burger sign over her head and winked conspiratorially at Janet. *Hypocrite*, she thought, embarrassed for a moment. But anything was OK when you were trying to get a creep like Janet out of the game. She jingled coins in her pocket. "Let's talk over a shake, OK? I'm buying."

Janet stroked her chin. "It's tempting," she said.

Tempting. Well, it was a start anyway. "What's your favorite flavor?" Amy asked hopefully.

Amy had told Janet that she was considering writing a story on the Unicorns for the school newspaper, which was a total lie but had gotten them to walk home from school together. She was determined to score a kill no matter what it took. She longed to scrawl a bright red X next to Janet's name. Especially after the way Janet had laughed about how she'd tricked Maria at lunchtime . . .

Janet yawned. "Strawberry, I guess."

"Mine too!" Amy lied. "Tell you what. Come on in with me, and I'll buy myself a shake. Then if you want one of your own—or just sips—it's yours!" She grinned at Janet, trying to ignore the unsettled feeling in your stomach that came when you ate one too many doughnuts.

On the heels of two too many candy bars, three too many chocolate drops, and so on.

Janet grinned back. "OK!" she agreed.

"Right this way!" Amy proclaimed, leading the way into the Dairi Burger.

This better work, she told herself grimly.

Already she felt like she'd gained twelve pounds.

"'My dearest Jessica,'" Steven said aloud, writing the words in long flowing script. He hunched over his desk and considered. "'I just wanted to say that . . .'"

He hesitated. "I love you" seemed too strong. "You're incredibly foxy"? Maybe. What had that cop said to the woman on *Homicide Plus!* last week? "Without you, my life wouldn't be worth living." He wrinkled his nose, remembering that Wednesday was the night *Homicide Plus!* came on. Keeping this resolution was *extremely* hard work.

Frowning, Steven stared at the paper in front of him and tapped his pen against the desk. A smile spread across his face. Of course! At the end of every *Phyllis Hartley* show, the announcer said, "Phyllis Hartley: At the heart of our lives!" in a hearty voice while Phyllis smiled and waved from the stage and the audience clapped enthusiastically.

"I just wanted to say that you're at the heart of my life!" he muttered, writing furiously. Who said that watching TV was a waste of time? His eyes sparkled. Skipping down a few lines on the page, he gave the paper a bold signature.

Eric Weinberg.

It was perfect. All he'd have to do would be to leave the paper where Elizabeth could see it and voilà!

Instant argument.

Pity he hadn't thought of it before.

"Oh, the candy store." Amy sighed. She put a dreamy expression on her face and tottered across the street. After the strawberry milk shake she seemed to be having some trouble keeping her balance. Pity she hadn't been able to get Janet to take even the tiniest taste. "Have you tried their fudge?"

"Not lately," Janet admitted. She walked along beside Amy. "Is it good?"

Amy swallowed hard. "Scrumptious," she said, hoping her eyes didn't appear glazed. "Want some? Um—I'll treat."

"That is *so* generous of you." Janet flashed Amy a

brilliant smile. "Maybe. It really sounds tempting."
She smacked her lips.

If I eat one more thing, I just may throw up, Amy
thought, breathing in slowly. *But it's all for a good
cause, isn't it?*

"Let's give it a try!" she said brightly, opening
the door and motioning Janet inside.

And now Jessica's turn. Steven chuckled under his
breath. He stared up at the ceiling. *Something—obvious. Something that'll really get Jess's goat.*

"Dear Elizabeth," he wrote. Short and simple,
that was the key. *Aha!* "Looking forward to our 'big
date' next week! *XXOO,* Eric."

Steven held up the paper and squinted at it.
Perfect.
Absolutely perfect.

He couldn't wait till the twins found the notes
he'd forged. Too bad he didn't have a video camera. It would be so awesome to send a tape of their
fight to *Totally Cool Home Videos.* Which was also on
tonight, he remembered . . .

He clenched his teeth tightly, trying not to think
about it.

First Janet had avoided Amy's milk shake. Then
she'd politely refused even a nibble of Amy's
fudge. Amy was beginning to notice a pattern here.

Still, it was worth trying one more time, right?

In her mind Amy ran through all the sweets she'd eaten that day. Ice cream, brownies, fudge, milk shakes, doughnuts . . . the list went on and on. And all to entice Janet into breaking her resolution. *For crying out loud, Janet, eat something!* she wanted to yell. A dizzy feeling swept up from her stomach, but she ignored it.

"I guess I just wasn't in the mood for mint peanut butter fudge," Janet chirped, tagging along down the street after Amy. "Funny. Usually I go for it in a big, big way."

Amy moaned. She'd only gotten the box of mint peanut butter fudge because Janet had said it was her favorite flavor. If it hadn't been, she'd have gotten something else. Like double chocolate. Or walnut.

Or nothing at all.

In the distance Amy could see the Some Crumb Bakery. She gagged at the sight. But it was too soon to admit defeat. "How about some pie, Janet?" she suggested.

"Mmm, pie!" Janet licked her lips. "I do like pie. . . ."

Yeah, well, you'd better! Amy thought, doggedly dragging herself down the sidewalk.

"What's this?" Elizabeth reached down and picked up a piece of paper from the couch. It had been folded neatly in half, and there was nothing on the outside to indicate what it was.

Curious, Elizabeth opened it. "Dear Jessica," she read, furrowing her eyebrows. "I just wanted to say that you're at the heart of my life." Her own heart skipped a beat as she saw the signature. *Eric Weinberg!*

Elizabeth blinked. Jealousy seized her. *Just wait till I get that Jessica,* she thought. She felt betrayed. A picture came into her mind: Jessica with her arm around Eric while Elizabeth looked on. . . .

Straightening up, she marched for Jessica's bedroom.

It was time to have a talk with her sister.

"I'm sorry, Amy," Janet said. "I guess I didn't want any of the pie." Her gaze rested wistfully on the almost finished slice in front of Amy. The two girls were sitting at a small table in the pie store. "It smelled real good, though, and you were so, um, *sweet* to offer me a piece."

"Thanks," Amy said thickly, resisting the urge to lie down and go to sleep. "I guess."

"Oh, my, look at the time!" Janet sprang to her feet. "I'd better get home right away!" She seized her purse and headed for the door. "See you tomorrow, Amy! And don't be late for school!"

"I—won't," Amy said slowly. Her stomach felt like an enormous basketball. With difficulty she stood up and leaned, swaying, against the table. Why had she eaten so much today? Why, why, why?

Because you were trying to trick Janet into eating

sweets, a voice inside her head told her.

And it hadn't even worked. Amy groaned, feeling ready to barf. Janet had resisted every temptation. They'd gone from one store to the next, and Janet hadn't eaten a *bite,* while *Amy* had eaten one thing after another and . . .

Amy blinked. She would have clapped her hand to her forehead if she'd felt strong enough. "It was a trick," she murmured, swallowing hard. "That creep! She . . ."

She rested her head in her hands. What a fool she'd been! She'd bet anything now that Janet had only been pretending to want something to eat. Just to get Amy all stuffed. What had Janet just said? "Don't be late for school!"

Because if Amy was late for school, then—

Suddenly there was a terrible taste in her mouth.

Amy didn't stop to finish her thought. Hurrying as quickly as she could, she waddled toward the bathroom.

Jessica frowned. What was that? She leaned over and picked up the scrap of paper lying outside the doorway to her room. Funny how she hadn't noticed it before. Unfolding it quickly, she looked at the top line.

"Dear Elizabeth," she read. "Looking forward to our 'big date' next week!"

Jessica blinked. *Our "big date," huh?* Her heart racing,

she hurried ahead to the signature. "*XXOO*, Eric."

Eric Weinberg! The paper fell from Jessica's grip. What nerve her sister had, sneaking around with Jessica's sort-of boyfriend! Even if he didn't know that was what he was yet! She marched onto the landing, ready to confront her sister.

And boy, oh boy, would she ever give Elizabeth a piece of her mind!

Here it comes, Steven thought, poking his head out of his bedroom. It was like a couple of trains coming together on the same track. He grinned as Jessica came down the stairs, a murderous look on her face, and Elizabeth came running up, her eyes flashing.

"Something wrong, girls?" he sang out.

"Something wrong? I'll say something's wrong!" Jessica snapped. She held out the note in her hand, her whole body shaking. "Elizabeth, I can't believe you—" But then she broke off and stopped suddenly in the middle of the staircase, and her gaze turned from the note to Steven.

"And as for you," Elizabeth hissed, "it makes me so incredibly angry that—" But she too halted in midsentence, lowered the note, and swung around to look at Steven.

Steven laughed nervously, wondering what was going on. It wouldn't count as a kill unless they finished their sentences. "Go on," he said carelessly. "Don't mind me."

Jessica took a deep breath. "Like I was saying," she said, "I can't believe you dropped this." She held out her piece of paper to Elizabeth.

Elizabeth's face relaxed into a grin. "And like I was saying," she added, "it makes me so incredibly angry that you might have lost this." She took Jessica's paper and handed the other one to her twin.

Rats. Steven made a face. *Sharked again!* "You mean you're not going to, you know, yell at each other?" he asked, hoping against hope that they were only putting on an act.

Elizabeth laughed and flung an arm around Jessica's shoulders. "Piece of advice, big brother," she said cheerfully.

"The next time you try to trick us with pretend love notes from Eric Weinberg, don't write them on stationery that says 'From the desk of Steven Wakefield' on the top!"

Nine

"Where's Amy?" Elizabeth hissed to Maria as the bell rang for school the next morning. She stared around the room. Other kids were taking their seats for homeroom, but there was no Amy.

"I don't know." Maria frowned. "I hope . . . well . . ." Her voice trailed off.

"I know what you mean." Elizabeth's palms felt slightly damp. She remembered that Amy had been planning to walk home with Janet yesterday afternoon—to tempt her into breaking her resolution. Elizabeth had expected a call from Amy later on that evening, but it hadn't come.

"If she's late—" Maria made a cutting motion with her forefinger across her throat.

Elizabeth nodded. If Amy was late, she was out of the game. She focused her gaze on the door to the classroom, willing Amy to suddenly appear.

But Amy didn't.

"OK, class, let's quiet down to a dull roar!" Mr. Bowman called from the front of the room.

Butterflies swarmed in Elizabeth's stomach. *Don't be silly*, she warned herself sternly. *Amy's late for school a lot of the time. And if she's only two or three minutes late, who's to know? She won't be zapped for that. . . .*

But deep down Elizabeth had the uncomfortable feeling that Amy wasn't going to be just a *few* minutes late.

And that Janet Howell had something to do with why she wasn't there yet.

"Three kills," Janet said sweetly at lunchtime. She tossed her scorecard across the table at Jessica. "Read 'em and weep."

Jessica frowned at the paper. *Three kills?* Lila with the bragging and Maria with the mirror, yeah, but three? Her eyes ran down the list and stopped at Amy's name, which had a neat red *X* drawn beside it. "Amy, huh?"

"She thought she could get me," Janet said with evident pride. "But I got her first. It just goes to show you, don't mess with a Howell. Want to know how I did it?"

"Um—" Jessica scratched her ear. Did she have a choice?

"Well, I won't go into the details," Janet said with a smirk. "Professional secrets and all that. Let's just say she was up half the night throwing up."

Jessica's stomach gave a lurch. "She—what?"

"You heard me," Janet said severely. "No, I didn't *poison* her or anything. And she's fine now. It's just that—" She lifted her eyebrows and bit into a tuna sandwich. "When you're up all night barfing—not that it ever happens to *me*, of course—your body takes, like, a while to recover."

Jessica's mouth hung open. She wasn't sure she could believe her ears. "Up all night *barfing?* What did you—"

"So poor Amy slept till about ten o'clock today. Which made her way late for school." Grinning wickedly, Janet extended her first finger. "*Zap!* Three confirmed kills."

"I see, Janet." Jessica couldn't help edging down the bench a little. She didn't like the look in Janet's eyes. Not at *all*. "Um—good for you."

"By my count, there aren't many of us left," Janet said. She ticked names off on her fingers. "Me, of course. Joe—for now. Your *brother*. Oh, yes, and the two of you." Narrowing her eyes, she stared at Jessica. "But that won't last long, I expect. You and your sister argue so often, I'm *sure* you won't make it till tomorrow night."

Jessica gulped. Janet's eyes seemed to bore in on her. It was strange the way Janet sounded almost—gleeful about the idea that the twins would break their resolution. *But you're supposed to be my friend*, she wanted to say. Only Janet was—well, Janet, so she didn't dare.

Janet tucked her scorecard back into her notebook

and smiled. "Three confirmed kills," she said happily. "And more to come."

And more to come. Jessica realized that she was holding her breath.

Why did she have the funny feeling that Jessica and Elizabeth Wakefield were next on Janet's kill list?

Just say, "Hi, Patty!" Joe Howell told himself, staring down the south corridor. It was after lunch, and Patty almost always walked this way from the cafeteria to her sixth-period class. *Just say, "Hi!" and take it from there and . . .*

His heart leaped. Was that her? No—just someone with hair a little like hers. He plastered a grin on his face and pulled himself up to his full height. *Confidence, that's the ticket,* he thought. *Look confident, act confident, and she'll be your date like that. Poof!* He snapped his fingers. It sounded so good, he did it again.

Nibbling his fingernails, he stared down the hall again. Two more dark-haired girls rounded the corner, then another and another. *Cut out the fingernails, Howell,* he told himself sternly, and whipped his hand behind his back. That was all he needed, to have her see him biting his nails like a kid. "Hi there, Patty," he rehearsed. He'd swing into step beside her, all suave and everything, and then start up a conversation, full of deep chuckles and intelligent comments like, "Well, the Lakers don't have the depth they used to," and she'd think he was, like, really cool and mature too and—

Joe bit his lip. Patty was coming. He took a deep breath, then another one. His heart pounded in his chest, and he stepped forward to intercept her. Just twenty more feet and—

Uh-oh. Joe stopped cold.

Just a few steps behind Patty was Steven Wakefield, hurrying along to class himself.

Bummer! Joe stepped back quickly as Patty approached. No way in the world was he going to take the chance of embarrassing himself in front of his buddy. What if Patty laughed in his face? What if she sneered and said, "Go out with—with *you?*" What if she just plain ignored him?

Well, if Wakefield saw, he'd never hear the end of it, that was for certain.

Joe pressed up against the wall and watched as Patty passed by.

Foolproof. Absolutely foolproof. Steven's eyes glittered as he emptied the contents of Jessica's makeup case into an old scuzzy plastic bag. It wasn't quite three o'clock, and the twins wouldn't be home from school for at least another few minutes.

He gave the makeup kit a shake to make sure it was empty. Then he reached into Elizabeth's rock-and-mineral box. *Good.* Gritty dirt clung to most of the specimens. With a nod of approval he grabbed a handful of dull gray stones and tossed them into the makeup case. He grinned to himself. Jessica was sure to hit the roof about *this* one.

Shoving the case onto Jessica's bed, Steven sauntered into Elizabeth's room and yanked open her sweater drawer. *Plenty of time,* he assured himself, and he fingered through the sweaters until he had found exactly the right one—a new blue crewneck that Elizabeth was especially proud of.

Bye, bye, resolution! he thought, pulling the sweater out of the drawer. With deft hands he wadded it up and walked with it to the bathroom. Turning both taps on full blast, he held the sweater beneath the running water until it was thoroughly soaked. *Maybe I should add some makeup stains?* he wondered, surveying the mess. Then he shook his head. This was enough. Casually he tossed the sodden sweater onto the bathroom floor. Just the kind of thing Jessica would do, he assured himself: borrow Elizabeth's sweater and get it all messed up.

Just like Elizabeth might get jealous and try to take over Jessica's makeup case for her stupid rocks and minerals.

Yup, the plan was foolproof. Totally foolproof. Steven nodded again, admiring his handiwork. He tiptoed back to his bedroom and flung himself facedown on his bed.

Let the fireworks begin!

I don't believe this, Elizabeth thought. She stood in the doorway of the bathroom, staring down at the

heap in front of her. Her teeth clenched and un-
clenched. *It's . . . it's my sweater, and Jess has gone and . . .*

And ruined it.

Bending to the floor, she grabbed the sweater
sleeves and pulled. The sweater flopped open, and
she could see the monogram EW on the chest.
Elizabeth felt like crying. *Typical Jess,* she thought
sorrowfully, shaking her head with anger and disap-
pointment. *Borrow my sweater and mess it up and . . .*

She massaged the back of her neck, but it didn't
make her feel any better.

*And worst of all, do it at a time when we have a
truce, so I can't even yell at her!*

*Since when is it my fault that she doesn't have a stu-
pid kit for her rocks and minerals?* Jessica asked herself, fury rising in her throat. She stared at the filthy
rocks scattered here and there in her makeup kit.
*Just because I have a sort-of case and she has only a shoe
box, that's no reason for her to . . .*

Jessica swallowed hard and banged the rocks
together helplessly. What a rotten, nasty thing for
her sister to do. She could feel the blood pounding
in her temples. It was typical Elizabeth, though.
To decide that *her* rocks and minerals were more
important than Jessica's own makeup . . .

She frowned.

And right now too. Elizabeth knew perfectly
well that Jessica wasn't going to say a word because

of their stupid resolution. Her twin had really caught her in the squeeze this time.

She slammed the lid of the kit shut. It just wasn't fair.

Seven . . . eight . . . nine . . . Elizabeth breathed deeply, filling her lungs with fresh, calming air.

Truce or no truce, she'd been on the verge of storming into her so-called sister's room and telling her off.

But she wanted that ski trip. And she didn't want those diapers.

So she'd decided to let her twin get away with it. This *once.*

Elizabeth breathed deeper. No way was *she* going to break the truce. She was going to be just as sweet and nice to Jessica as she could.

Even if it *killed* her.

Thirteen . . . fourteen . . . fifteen . . .

Twenty-three . . . twenty-four . . . twenty-five . . . Jessica sat on her bed, facing the wall and breathing so deeply, her lungs ached.

She longed to run to her stupid sister's room and start throwing stupid rocks and minerals at Elizabeth's stupid head.

But she wouldn't. She'd be mature. She'd be calm and collected and not let Elizabeth push her over the edge.

So she'd stay in here, taking deep breaths and

thinking mature thoughts until she was ready to come out.

Even if it took till next Tuesday.

Twenty-nine . . . thirty . . . thirty-one . . .

Steven frowned. It was entirely too quiet to suit him. Surely the girls would have noticed by now. Standing up, he walked to the doorway of his room just in time to see the twins heading down the stairs together, hand in hand.

"How about a snack?" Elizabeth was asking Jessica.

"Sure," Jessica replied. "I'll make some popcorn?"

Steven swallowed hard. "Um—guys?" he called. "Did you—I mean—" He couldn't very well say exactly what was on his mind, or they'd know he was the culprit. "I mean—um—"

His gaze lit on the door to Jessica's room. There was the makeup kit, open wide, with rocks spilled onto the floor. He blinked. And on the floor next to Elizabeth's room was—the sweater. Stretched out and drying. So they knew.

And they weren't killing each other over it.

"Did you want to say something, Steven?" Elizabeth asked impatiently.

Steven shook his head and managed a weak smile. "Never mind," he said. "Nothing—important." He watched the twins till they were out of sight down the stairs.

Now what?

Ten

Steven punched in Joe's number and held the phone to his ear. If Howell couldn't give him some advice about dealing with the twins, no one could. Which would be a real shame, because the last thing he wanted was to be cooped up with his dorky sisters on the ski trip and—

There was a metallic click. "Hi, you've reached the Howell residence," Mrs. Howell's voice said into the receiver. "No one is here to take your call right now, but if you leave your name, number, and a short message, we'll—"

Something rattled. "Hello?" a girl's voice interrupted.

"—back to you," the voice finished. There was a beep.

"Hello!" the girl sang out, louder this time.

Janet. Steven rolled his eyes. "Is Joe there?" he barked.

"No," Janet snapped. "And I don't know where he is either. Or when he'll be back. Who is this?"

"Steven," Steven said, leaning back in his chair. "Wakefield. Hi, Janet," he added to be polite. "I'll try again later—"

"Steven Wakefield," Janet said thoughtfully. "You know . . . I was just thinking about you."

That was a switch. "You—what?" Steven narrowed his eyes.

"Not like *that*, dummy," Janet scoffed. "No, I was thinking about you and your sisters. Ever seen them in diapers?"

Steven snorted. "Not since they were babies." Was this a hint of some kind? "Um—what do you mean, Janet?"

"Are all the Wakefields as slow as you are?" Janet demanded. "All I meant was that it would be very cool to see them wearing diapers to the party tomorrow. Do you agree?"

Do I agree? Are you out of your tree? Steven ran his hand through his hair. "Uh—now that you mention it," he admitted, "yeah, that would be pretty neat." *Play it cool, Wakefield,* he told himself, but he could feel his stomach starting to churn with excitement. "Did you have something in mind?"

Janet sighed loudly. "Something in mind?" she mimicked. "Look. It's really important to me to be the only well-dressed girl at the party so I can dance with . . ." Her voice trailed off. "Well. Never mind who. The point is, your sisters are in the way. So if you have any ideas—" She paused meaningfully, and silence hung in the air. "I might be willing to help out."

Steven pursed his lips. "It's Eric Weinberg, isn't it?"

"Who told you that?" Janet's voice was shrill.

"No one." Steven grinned to himself. And she'd said Wakefields were slow. His heart beat faster. "Listen, Janet. Um—I don't exactly know how to say this. But I've tried to get them to argue, and nothing's worked." His mind raced. "But I tell you what. I've got a new idea, and if *we* can get them to fight, I'll arrange a date for you and Eric."

There was a long pause. "You?" Janet said.

"Yeah, me!" Steven retorted. "I know his sister, Patty. Patty and me, we're like *this.*" He pressed his first two fingers together, forgetting that Janet couldn't see them through the phone. "Anyway, that's a promise, OK? You get them to fight, and I'll—set you up with Eric." *Somehow.*

"Well." Janet clicked her tongue. "A double date. You and Patty, me and Eric. How sweet. You'd pay, of course."

"Of course," Steven echoed weakly.

There was a pause. "I suppose it's worth a try," Janet said at last. "So what are *we* going to do?"

"Divide and conquer," Steven said slowly. "Here's the plan. . . ."

"I'm home!"

Joe burst in through the front door of his house. He'd spent the afternoon doing some heavy-duty studying in the library. At last he'd gotten those stupid irregular German verbs under control. . . . He crossed to the refrigerator and grabbed a can of soda. "Anybody here?"

No one answered.

Guess they're all gone. Joe popped open the lid of the can and took a long drink. He considered scooping some ice cream to go with the soda. After all that studying, he deserved a treat. And since Casey's was definitely out—

Casey's. His mouth began to water. Suddenly he had an enormous urge for a Super Sundae. Taking a deep breath, he drank another gulp of soda—and noticed that the red message light on the answering machine was blinking.

Could be for me, he thought, and pressed the play button. The machine whirred and rewound. There was a click, and the tape began to play.

"Hello?"

Joe frowned. *Janet's voice.*

"Is Joe there?" Steven Wakefield asked. At least Joe *thought* it was Wakefield.

"No," Janet snapped, sounding tinny through

the tape player. "And I don't know where he is either. Or when he'll be back. Who is this?"

"Steven," Steven said.

Joe rolled his eyes. Somehow his sister had recorded the whole stupid conversation. Probably she'd been up in her room or something and had answered the phone up there—right about the time the answering machine got it. He nodded slowly. *Yeah. That would do it, all right.* Once the machine got started, it would just keep recording whatever came through the wires unless you pressed stop. Which she couldn't do if she was upstairs and the machine was downstairs. He sighed impatiently, barely paying attention as the conversation rolled on. *Typical Janet. She's so stupid, she wouldn't notice if—*

Wait a minute.

Joe leaned toward the tape, his heart hammering. What had his sister just said? Stopping the tape, he rewound it a little and pushed play.

"If *we* can get them to fight, I'll arrange a date for you and Eric." *Steven's voice.*

"You?" Janet sounded even more sarcastic than usual.

Steven muttered something. "Patty and me, we're like *this.*"

Joe took a deep breath. He could just see his friend holding up two fingers pressed tightly together. . . .

"A double date," Janet mused. "You and Patty, me and Eric . . ."

Joe's forefinger itched to stab the off button. But he forced himself to listen to the whole message straight through first. *And I thought we were friends,* he told himself grimly. The Wakefield on the phone right now was no friend of his, that was for sure. He tensed his body. If Steven was plotting with Joe's own stupid *sister* to take away the girl of Joe's dreams . . . well, this meant war.

"So," Steven was saying. "The moment I get off the phone, you call for Jessica. Do what we planned. I'll work on Elizabeth."

"It could work," Janet said slowly. "So, um, I'll see you at the mall."

"At the mall," Steven agreed.

"And button your lip," Janet reminded him. "Not a word to anyone." There was a pause. "Especially not my stupid *brother.*"

Tell her off, Wakefield, Joe begged silently, but deep down he suspected that Wakefield wouldn't.

Steven laughed easily. "OK," he promised.

You jerk. Joe's eyes clouded over. The machine clicked off. *You should never have let her get away with that.* Grabbing his jacket, he headed for the door. Now it was war for sure.

Let's see how impressed Patty's going to be when she sees you in a diaper! he thought.

*   *   *

"You know, Elizabeth," Steven remarked, "the Unicorns think you're pretty dorky, the way you spend all your time with rocks and minerals."

Elizabeth eyed him curiously. "Why are you telling me this?"

"Oh, no reason," Steven lied. He grinned. "Just that I didn't tell anybody we were going to the rock-and-mineral show together."

"You couldn't have," Elizabeth pointed out. "It opened today, and you only invited me five minutes before we left, and—"

"I didn't tell *anybody*," Steven interrupted. Who cared about facts anyway? "Except Jessica. But I didn't tell any *other* Unicorns because they'd just laugh. Which would make you mad," he added carelessly.

"Uh-huh." Elizabeth frowned. "So, um, what's your point?"

"No point," Steven said happily, walking on toward the mall.

This plan was absolutely foolproof. Oh, he knew he'd used that word before, but this time it really was. He and Janet had worked it out to the last detail. Right now Janet was walking to the mall with Jessica and some of the other Unicorns. She'd lead them right to the rock-and-mineral show and start making cutting remarks about Elizabeth and her dorky interests.

And what was Elizabeth going to think? That

Jessica brought the Unicorns there just to make fun of her. And if she didn't, Steven himself would start dropping hints.

Foolproof. Steven grinned to himself and quickened his pace.

Joe broke into a run. His only chance was to get to the mall before his sister and Steven could put their plan into action. *Janet and Steven. Boy. What a combo!* He darted left at an intersection, barely missing a kid on a bicycle. *Couple of two-faced, lying little—*

And the darnedest thing was, now *he* had to rely on Wakefield's little sisters to bail him out of this mess. If they could hold it together, and if he could convince them that they needed to join with him, well, they had a chance.

Otherwise it'd be diapers for the twins.

And Patty would wind up with Steven.

Joe puffed around the next corner. His mouth felt dry, but he urged his legs on.

Oh, man, did he ever need a Super Sundae from Casey's now!

"Look at *that*." Janet's voice dripped sarcasm. "Yes, sirree, if you want to know all about minerals, you should go see Elizabeth 'Rocks on the Brain' Wakefield."

"The middle school's own rock expert," Lila said with a sneer. "Everything you never wanted to know about rocks. Know what she said in class the other day?"

Elizabeth stood stock-still in front of a display of geodes. *Where did they come from?* she wondered, flicking her eyes over the group to see if her sister was there. There was a sinking feeling in her stomach.

"Look, Jessica," Janet said sharply. "Your very own sister, playing with rocks. How old did you say she was? Three?"

"Two and a half?" Ellen Riteman giggled.

"Oh, Jessica," Steven murmured, theatrically pressing his hand to his forehead. "I *told* you not to tell anybody. Now you've gone and—" He broke off.

Elizabeth blinked. So Jessica *was* to blame. *Great.* Here she was, the laughingstock of the Unicorn Club because her sister had been so obnoxious. She glared at her twin. *If looks could kill, I'd be minus one sister.*

"Gee, look at that little brown rock," Janet said in a baby voice. "I bet it has a long, fancy-schmantzy name. Like *stupid-brownilus dumb-elizabethus.*" She elbowed Jessica in the ribs. "Don't you agree, Jessica?"

"Well, as a matter of fact," Jessica said, stepping forward. Her eyes met Elizabeth's. "I think—I think rocks are actually . . . interesting."

"You do?" Janet gasped.

"You *do?*" Steven echoed, looking worried.

Elizabeth didn't know what to think. But who was she to turn down her sister's help? "I've got a great idea!" she said loudly, wrapping her arm tightly around her twin's shoulders. "Why don't we give them a guided tour of the rock show together?"

Jessica grinned. "You're on!" she said with feeling.

It's all your fault, Steven thought, grumbling. He glanced angrily at Janet. If she hadn't come on so strong, maybe the plan would have worked. *Stupid-brownilus dumb-elizabethus. Yeah, right.*

He filled his cheeks with air and blew out sharply. Of course, maybe he'd been a little, well, *obvious* about how Jessica was the only person who knew where he and Elizabeth were going. Maybe he'd been a little to blame. A *little*.

But mostly it was Janet's fault.

". . . and in this case," Elizabeth was saying proudly, "you can see five pieces of tigereye! Notice the stripes especially. Aren't they lovely?"

Steven growled and stared daggers at Janet. She could go *rot* for all he cared. So much for cooperation.

Just *see* if he fixed her up with Eric when he invited Patty to the party.

Jessica scowled. Joining forces with Elizabeth had seemed like a good idea at the time. She wasn't quite sure who was up to what, but something sure smelled fishy. The way Janet had called up out of the blue and demanded that Jessica be ready in ten minutes . . . and how she'd steered them to the mineral show instead of where the rest of the Unicorns really wanted to go . . . and why was Steven here with Elizabeth anyway? It was all very mysterious, and she couldn't shake the suspicion that somehow the twins were being set up.

So of course, joining with Elizabeth made the most sense.

But if Elizabeth was going to point out every detail on every single rock in the entire show, she thought she just might barf. So who *cared* if the Mohs' scale told how hard a rock was? And who really *cared* if you needed calcium and iron to live?

"This is a *nice* rock," Elizabeth said with a grin, touching a gray stone. "That's a joke. Its name is pronounced 'nice,' but it's spelled *gneiss*. The *g* is silent. Gneiss, nice. Get it?" She laughed.

Jessica gritted her teeth. She wasn't exactly sorry that she hadn't joined in teasing her sister. But things couldn't go on like this.

Quickly she made a decision.

"And this one—" Elizabeth reached for a hunk of shale. It was so cool to have people listening to her talk about rocks. Somehow she had the idea that most of the time when she talked about her hobby, people's eyes just glazed over. *But now I can show them how interesting rocks really are.* "This is a piece of a rock known as—"

"My turn," Jessica said suddenly, pushing Elizabeth out of the way. She picked up a piece of sandstone. "This rock is known as George," she said, turning it in her hands. "Say hi, George."

"Hi, George," Ellen dutifully repeated.

Elizabeth laughed nervously. "It's actually sandstone," she told her sister. "You can see how the rock is put together by—"

"Sandstone, sure," Jessica said airily. "But I like to call it George. If you give rocks names, they listen to you better. I've noticed that."

Elizabeth forced a smile on her face. "Ha, ha, Jessica. Now if you'll look over here—" She motioned to a pile of jasper quartz. "Notice how when the light hits—"

"It's really cool when the light hits it," Jessica interrupted. "I've, like, noticed that too. But you know what happens when a *sledgehammer* hits it?"

"As I was saying . . ." Elizabeth tried not to sound annoyed.

"Boom! Little pieces all over," Jessica said. "Rocks break, did you know that? Most of the time anyway. Which reminds me, do you know which rock they named rock and roll music after?"

Elizabeth took a deep breath.

It was going to be very hard to keep from bashing her sister's head in with a geode.

But in the interests of family harmony—and no diapers—she'd do her best.

Eleven

"And this is an amethyst over here," Elizabeth said doggedly, trying to ignore the snickers from Ellen and Lila. She wished she'd never come to the rock-and-mineral show to begin with. "You can tell an amethyst by the color—"

"I think we've had about enough rocks for one day," Jessica interrupted. "Anybody for Casey's?"

"Casey's!" Lila smacked her lips.

Janet's eyes flashed. "Good idea, Jessica," she said. "I think this little lecture has gone on long enough. I won't eat anything, of *course*, but if the rest of you would like to come . . ." She shot Steven a furious look. "*He's* buying."

"I—am?" Steven swallowed hard.

"I believe that's what you *promised*," Janet said frostily.

Steven blinked. "Oh. Um—yeah." He groped for his back pocket. "Right."

Elizabeth drew in a deep breath. She could hear her sister's voice echoing in her head: "You can do a lot of stuff with rocks. Like, you can build a wall if you have enough of them. Or make a paperweight. Or skip them over a lake."

"Don't you have enough *money?*" Janet demanded, raising an eyebrow ever so slightly.

Steven looked as if he were calculating in his head. "Um—" He hesitated. "I guess I could swing it. If you all, like, keep it simple." He turned to Elizabeth. "You won't be coming, right, sis?" he asked almost pleadingly. "I mean, these aren't exactly your best friends. . . ." He scratched the back of his neck.

After you got me into this? Elizabeth gave a snort. "Oh, I think I'll come along," she said sweetly. Wild horses couldn't keep her away. Even if she had to sit with the Unicorns and her so-called brother. A milk shake from Casey's was exactly what she needed. A chance to cool down with a nice cold chocolate chip shake . . .

Mmm.

Licking her lips in anticipation, Elizabeth followed the crowd as they headed for Casey's.

"One chocolate chip milk shake, please," Jessica said to old Mr. Casey. She sat in a booth with Janet,

Lila, and Kimberly; Elizabeth, she saw, had gone to the counter and was swinging slowly back and forth on one of the old-fashioned stools. As for Steven, he was sitting glumly at a table by himself, stacking coins in small piles in front of him.

Jessica drew in the smell of ice cream. In the background catchy ragtime music played, and a ceiling fan buzzed slowly. Already she felt calmer.

Mr. Casey's eyes twinkled. "Coming right up."

"Thanks." Jessica shut her eyes and listened to the sound of the music. Oh, boy, did she ever need a relaxing shake from Casey's. Dealing with Elizabeth was hard work. A couple of times there at the mineral show she'd thought she was about to go postal on her twin, but she hadn't.

Which meant the ski trip was still on. Leaning against the tabletop, Jessica breathed a sigh of relief.

The mineral exhibit, the mineral exhibit . . . Joe picked up speed through the mall. His side ached, but he paid no attention. He *had* to get to the twins before Janet and Steven got them to argue. The idea of Steven getting Patty and Janet *winning*—well, it was too much for a guy to take. He dashed past the Cineplex, past Chez Foot and the sporting goods store, past Casey's, past—

Whoa!

Quickly Joe dug his heels into the tiled floor. His arms backpaddled for balance. He turned around, bumping a guy in a Ratshark T-shirt, and stared behind him.

The twins were *there*. In Casey's. And sitting apart from each other. Joe started for the door but then hesitated.

After all, he'd resolved not to set *foot* in Casey's. Not for any reason at all.

His chest heaving, he stood just outside the doorway, staring in.

"Didn't I just serve you a chocolate chip shake?" old Mr. Casey asked, his bright blue eyes sparkling as he took Elizabeth's order.

"Um—no." Elizabeth sat up straight. What did Mr. Casey mean?

Mr. Casey laughed to show he was only kidding. "Your sister's here. Did you know that? She ordered the exact same thing. I guess it's true what they say about identical twins and—"

"She *what?*" The words came out before Elizabeth could stop them. Her chest felt tight, and for a moment she thought she couldn't breathe. "My *sister* ordered a chocolate chip milk shake *too?*"

Mr. Casey backed away. "That's right."

Elizabeth twisted her napkin angrily in her lap. The nerve of that Jessica. After everything else, ordering the exact same thing at Casey's! She didn't know why it was bugging her so much, but it was. She slid down from the stool.

"Hey, Jessica!" she called. *What a copycat.*

Jessica's head jerked up. "What do you want?" she asked, getting to her feet.

This is it, Elizabeth thought. Her heart pounded. Slowly she walked toward her sister. "I just wanted to talk to you for a moment. In the corner over there," she added quickly. Mad as she was, she didn't want Janet to see them arguing.

Jessica rolled her eyes, but she followed. Elizabeth could see Janet staring intently at them as they walked away. "So what's this all about, huh, Elizabeth?" Jessica demanded when they were safely out of earshot.

Elizabeth took a deep breath. "I just wanted to know why you were being such a copycat?" she said in a clear voice.

"A copycat?" Jessica curled her lip. "What are you talking about?" Slowly and deliberately she stepped toward her sister.

In the distance Elizabeth could see Janet sitting straight up, a catlike expression on her face, but she couldn't seem to stop herself. "You know perfectly well what I'm talking about," she snapped. "I was going to order a chocolate chip milk shake and—"

"Oh, like it's your *property?*" Jessica said, staring hard at her twin. "Like you made up the recipe or something?"

"That has nothing to do with it." Elizabeth

clenched her jaw. "The point is, you have no business copycatting me."

Jessica snorted. "*I* ordered *mine* first. Listen, Elizabeth, I am sick and tired of you and your—"

"Well, I'm even sicker and tireder than that!" Elizabeth could hear her voice rising. She put her hand two inches above her head. "I've had it up to *here* with you."

"Talk about up to *here*," Jessica began, holding her hand about a foot above her own head.

Out of the corner of her eye Elizabeth could see Janet looking their way, but she didn't even care. Right now Jessica being a copycat was the most important thing in her entire life. "Copycatting again," she said, blinking furiously. "See? You always copycat, and I'm tired of that too, and—"

"Hey!" There was a sudden movement, and all at once Joe Howell was standing between the twins, his arms outstretched. "Are you guys *nuts* or what?"

"She started it," Jessica said sulkily. She tried to lean around Joe, but his strong arms held her back.

"I did not either!" Elizabeth put her hands on her hips, barely taking the time to wonder where Joe had come from.

"I don't care who started it," Joe admonished them. "The point is, you guys can't blow it. If you argue—" He stopped for a deep breath. "Then Janet wins. And so does Steven. Did you know they've been plotting against you?"

"They—have?" Elizabeth's hand flew to her mouth.

"They sure have," Joe assured her. "My sister wants to make sure she's the only girl not in diapers at this party. And as for Steven, he's willing to help her out."

"Steven and—Janet?" Jessica croaked. "You have *got* to be kidding."

"Bizarre," Joe said wryly. "But true." His voice took on a sense of urgency. "Listen. Two things. First, don't give in. And second, two can play at that game. Or maybe even three."

Elizabeth's body relaxed a little. "You mean—you'd work with us?" she asked dubiously. It was hard to know if she trusted Joe or not. "I—I don't know, Jess. What do you think?"

Jessica hesitated. "I don't know if Casey's is the best place to be thinking—"

"Casey's!" Joe gasped. "Oh, man, I completely forgot. Listen, we can talk later. I'd better get out of here before—"

"*Zap!*" a loud voice interrupted.

Elizabeth whirled to the table where Jessica had been sitting. Janet was standing beside it, a triumphant look in her eyes, her forefinger pointing directly at Joe.

"Oh, man." Joe sighed and hung his head.

"Unlawful entry of Casey's," Janet proclaimed. "Four confirmed kills!"

* * *

Joe sat at home, staring out into the darkness. Night had fallen, and he still couldn't believe his bad luck.

Busted for going into Casey's. He hadn't been eating a sundae, hadn't even ordered one. Hadn't even been *going* to order one. All he'd done was step in there to break up a fight. To help out the Wakefield twins. To do a good deed.

And all it had gotten him was—a diaper.

His jaw tightened. Outside, a motorcycle's headlights raced by, a single beam of light piercing the night. So now only Steven was left. Plus Janet and the twins.

And as for Steven and especially Janet—well, he wanted nothing more than to put a nice big red *X* on his own scorecard next to their names. To jump out from behind the bushes or someplace and yell, "*Zap!* Two confirmed kills." Then maybe he'd blow the smoke away from his forefinger like an Old West gunslinger. . . .

He frowned. What had he said to the twins? Something about Janet wanting to be the only well-dressed girl at the party. Why was that? To attract What's-his-name, Patty's brother. Eric.

A little light went on in Joe's mind. He sat straight up.

It could work.

And it wasn't like he had anything left to lose either.

He reached for the telephone book and leafed through to the *W*s.

"Think it'll work?" Elizabeth whispered.

"Of course it'll work," Jessica answered with more confidence than she felt. She stood in the living room, a videotape in her hand. "It *has* to work." After what her brother had tried to do to them, it had *better* work, she thought grimly. "You're on," she hissed.

Elizabeth paled and nodded. "Um—so that sure was a great movie we just saw this evening."

"Oh, it was a *great* movie," Jessica assured her loudly. She listened for signs of Steven in the rec room downstairs. *"A really great movie,"* she repeated even louder. *"With blood and guts and stuff like that."*

Something stirred in the rec room. Jessica grinned. "Yeah, a friend loaned it to me," she half shouted.

"So, um, when do you have to give it back?" Elizabeth asked, raising her voice.

"Tomorrow morning at school," Jessica complained. There was a squeak on the downstairs steps. "Bummer, huh?"

"Really," Elizabeth agreed. "That part with the helicopter and the, um—" She looked blankly at Jessica.

"The helicopter and the frogman," Jessica supplied. *There. That ought to get Steven interested.* "And the escape from the jail cell," she added quickly. "When there were a million bombs going off all over the place?" She waved the videotape in the air. It was just an ordinary tape of *Days of Turmoil*, her favorite soap opera, but Steven didn't need to know that. "The babes," she hissed to Elizabeth.

"Oh—right." Elizabeth licked her lips. "And the babes," she said loudly. "They were so, like, um, pretty."

"And all those funny lines!" Jessica chuckled. "Remember the part where, um, that guy said—" She couldn't come up with a line that was funny enough, so she burst into hysterical laughter instead.

"Oh, *yeah*, that part," Elizabeth said, joining in. "And the part where—" She broke off, giggling. "Oh, it was too funny."

Out of the corner of her eye Jessica saw her brother's head poke up on the stairway. *The trap's been set*, she thought happily. *Now for the bait.*

"Well, I'm *so* glad we watched it," she exclaimed, wiping imaginary tears from her eyes. "Guess I'll put it here on the table so I won't forget it tomorrow." She scowled ferociously at her sister.

"Oh—um, it really has to go back *tomorrow?*" Elizabeth asked wistfully.

"Afraid so." Jessica set down the tape. "Guess we'd better head for bed." She faked a yawn. "What a movie, though. Makes Arnold Weissenhammer films seem so—so *boring*."

Taking Elizabeth's arm, she left the room.

Bait—check, she thought happily. *Trap—check. Now all we need is our brother to play the mouse!*

*   *   *

"Well, that'll be great, Eric," Joe said heartily into the phone. He listened for a moment. "I know she'll really appreciate it. Just don't tell her I gave you the idea, OK?"

Joe grinned out into the darkness, which suddenly didn't seem so dark anymore. Not to gloat or anything, but this plan seemed as idiot-proof as could be. He truly didn't see any way it could go wrong.

"You can count on me," Eric promised. "And, um, thanks a lot for the tip, Joe."

"Anytime." Joe breathed deeply. He felt good—good all over. Confident. Like everything he touched was turning into gold. It was like they said: If life hands you a lemon, make lemonade. Confidence, that was the ticket.

Confidence. Joe gripped the phone tighter. He'd just had an idea. Well—why not? "Hey, Eric," he continued, trying to sound as if it was no big deal, "is your sister around? You know, Patty?"

"Patty?" Eric sounded surprised. "I think so. Just a minute. I'll check."

The phone was set down. Joe leaned back in his seat, thinking confident thoughts. *You can do this,* he assured himself. *No problemo. Be suave. Debonair. Sweep her off her feet.* He concentrated on deep, even breaths. *In, out, in, out—*

"Hello?"

Joe filled his lungs with air. "Hi, Patty," he said,

pleased that he was speaking in his own normal voice rather than in squeaks. "This is Joe. Howell. I met you at Casey's?"

There was a pause. "Oh!" Patty said, sounding pleased. "Hi, Joe. What's up?"

Joe began to grin. "Listen," he said, "I was just wondering . . ."

Steven stepped through the quiet house in his pajamas, trying to make as little noise as possible. Too bad Jessica's borrowed tape had to go back to her friend tomorrow. He'd have preferred to wait and watch it a couple of days from now, after the party, but desperate times called for desperate measures.

By the light of the moon Steven reached for the tape. He turned the box this way and that, but he couldn't quite make out the name of the movie. Still, if it had bombs and helicopters and babes and put Weissenhammer to shame, well . . .

He froze, listening intently. Was that a creak on the staircase? *One one-thousand, two one-thousand, three one-thousand . . .*

No, there wasn't a sound.

Steven managed a faint grin. *Only a guilty conscience,* he told himself. He inserted the tape in the VCR and punched the on button on the remote. Immediately he pushed the volume down as low as possible. It wouldn't do to have the twins come running down in their nightgowns and bust him.

The screen flickered on. *The Extra-Late Show* with Daniel Betterman. Steven itched to turn up the volume to hear what jokes Betterman was cracking, but he didn't dare. He stared at the screen. It had been a long time since he'd watched, and he'd really missed it. Still, it wasn't Betterman he'd come down here to see. No, it was Jessica's tape. With his thumb he pressed play.

Betterman vanished. A few seconds of static appeared on the screen, and then that gave way to a bright blue background. Steven yawned and settled down in a chair to watch. *This better be good*, he thought sullenly.

The background melted away slowly. The words *Days of Turmoil: Episode #9,536* stood out in bold letters.

"What?" Steven jumped up. *It's a trick!* his mind screamed. But before he could react, there was a click. Light flooded the room. Steven blinked and swung around, knowing in his heart of hearts what he would see and hear.

"*Zap!*" Elizabeth and Jessica hissed, standing up behind a couch. Their forefingers were extended—directly at him.

"A confirmed kill for the Wakefield sisters!" Jessica exulted, high-fiving Elizabeth.

Steven stared bleakly at the TV set.

Sharked again! he thought, a hollow feeling in his stomach.

And for Days of Turmoil *too!*

Twelve

"Three people left," Janet said meaningfully. She pushed a stray piece of hair behind her ear and stared down at Jessica and Elizabeth from the top of a ladder. "Pretty soon we'll be down to one."

Elizabeth licked her lips nervously. *I will not argue with my sister,* she repeated for what seemed like the millionth time. It was Friday afternoon, just a few hours before the party, and the twins were helping Janet and Joe hang the decorations for that evening. "We'll see, Janet," she said quietly, and she stuck a balloon to the wall with a piece of masking tape.

"It was interesting what happened at study hall," Janet added. She wound a purple streamer around a light fixture. "*Someone* left a big box of candy on my desk. With a note on it that said 'Sweets for the Sweet, Love Always, Denny.'" Her eyes flashed.

"Well, of course, I can't eat sweets *now*. So I gave the box to Mrs. Lister because Mr. Bowman said it was her birthday. Only without the card, naturally."

"Naturally," Elizabeth echoed with a sigh. She tore off another piece of tape. It was too bad the box of candy from "Denny" hadn't worked. The box had been a last-ditch effort by Jessica, Lila, Amy, Maria, and Elizabeth herself, and for a moment Elizabeth had thought it might actually do the trick. They'd watched with bated breath as Janet had slid the lid off the box and actually picked up two of the caramels. . . .

But then Eric Weinberg had come into the room, and Janet had shut the box with a thud.

"You mean the box wasn't from Denny?" Jessica asked. She moved a couch into a corner with Joe's help and stared innocently at Janet.

"Of *course* not," Janet snapped. "Hand me that stapler, Elizabeth. I knew it all along. Especially when I saw Denny walking through the halls after lunch with his arm wrapped around someone who doesn't have any of my charms." With a vicious thwack she stapled the streamer to itself.

A smile played at Elizabeth's lips. It was nice to see Janet bested for a change.

"Still," Janet said with a contented sigh, "it's just as well, I guess. Denny was too *boring*, if you know what I mean. Our relationship was stale. Predictable. And I have a new boyfriend now," she added after a pause. Leaning over the ladder's edge toward Elizabeth and Jessica, she grinned a terrible grin. "Perhaps you know him. His name's Eric."

Don't react. Elizabeth tried to ignore the chill she suddenly felt. "Would that be, um, Eric Weinberg?" she asked. Behind her Jessica gave a sharp intake of breath.

"Eric Weinberg, that's right," Janet said, obviously enjoying herself. She scampered down the ladder, her eyes twinkling. "I'd been relying on, um, somebody else to get me a date with him, but, well, that fell through. You can't trust a Wakefield, I guess. So I deep-sixed *that* idea and called him myself. He'll be my date tonight." She smiled triumphantly. "I *might* share him. Perhaps for one dance each."

"Very generous," Joe said with a nod. Elizabeth stared at him in surprise. It was about the first time he'd spoken all afternoon. "Like I always say, my sister's just the very model of generosity."

"Um—thanks." Janet eyed her brother suspiciously. "I think. You're not being sarcastic, are you?"

"Who, me?" Joe asked, thumping his chest. "Surely you jest."

The doorbell rang. "I'll get it!" Joe called out, and he disappeared from the room quicker than Elizabeth thought possible.

"He was just being sarcastic," Janet said with a heavy sigh. "Though it's a known fact that I *am* one of the most generous people in the whole school.

Like the way I gave Mrs. Lister my chocolates today. She even said so. She said to me, 'Why, Janet, what a generous girl you are!'"

Elizabeth shook her head. If Janet was generous, well, she'd hate to meet someone who was selfish.

"Someone for you, sis," Joe called out in a perky voice. He stepped back into the living room, a huge grin on his face, and motioned toward Janet. "There she is, kid. He says he knows you," he added to Janet.

Elizabeth blinked. Eric Weinberg stood in the doorway to the living room, smiling broadly. "Hi, Janet," he said in a friendly voice.

"Eric!" Janet beamed at him. She crossed the room and rested her hand on his arm. *As if he's her toy,* Elizabeth thought with distaste. "I'm *so* happy to see you! Did you come to help set up, or did you just want to say hi?" Fluttering her eyelashes, she guided Eric gently into the room.

Gag! Elizabeth wrinkled her nose. Janet was being absolutely nauseating, and when Elizabeth looked at Jessica's face, she could tell that her twin was thinking about the same thing.

"Well—a little of both," Eric said shyly. He sketched a wave to the twins. "Hi, Elizabeth. Hi, Jessica. I'll get you straight one of these days, you'll see."

"Don't bother about *them,*" Janet sang out. "Sit down, Eric. Make yourself at home."

Joe cleared his throat. "I think, um, Eric has

something for you," he said, pointing to a red coffee can tucked under Eric's arm.

"Oh, this!" Eric leaped as if he'd been stung and flashed Janet a grin. "Almost forgot. Listen, I'm pretty famous for my chocolate chip cookies, OK? At least I was around my old school and—" He paused and rubbed his cheek, which was turning faintly red. "Oh, whatever! I made you a batch of cookies." With a quick motion he held out the can to Janet.

Janet stood stock-still. "Oh, how sweet," she said, smiling with her mouth. But not, Elizabeth noticed, with her eyes.

Eric pried the plastic lid off the can. "Mmm," he said, taking a deep breath. "They're, like, fresh baked. It's not real often you see a guy who likes to make cookies and stuff, but it's a talent of mine. Have one!"

"Yeah, have one, Janet," Joe murmured, his eyes shining. "Have two."

"Thanks!" Janet swallowed hard. Swiftly she took the can from Eric and set it on a table. "These are, um, so great, Eric, I want to save them for the party tonight. It would be so, um, *generous* to share them with everybody else and—"

"Oh, don't do *that!*" Eric shifted uncomfortably. "I made another batch for the party. But I made this one just for you. It's my secret recipe and everything."

Janet laughed nervously. "You're so sweet, Eric," she said, linking hands with him. "But I just can't. I—I just can't," she finished lamely.

Elizabeth leaned forward, her palms growing slightly sweaty. She smiled. It would be so easy for Janet if she could just tell Eric about the game, but Janet was the one who made the rule about no telling. . . . Elizabeth hardly dared to breathe. *Eat them, eat them,* she repeated under her breath.

"Aw, c'mon, sis," Joe drawled. "Have a bite. It won't kill you."

"Of course it won't *kill* me, Joe!" Janet gulped and gave a hollow chuckle. "It's just that . . . that . . ." She hesitated.

Eric frowned. "I insist," he said. "It wouldn't be fair for me to even show up tonight as your guest if you didn't take one now. Anyway, I hope you're not one of those *boring* girls who never eat sweets." He laughed lightly, but Elizabeth could tell there was an undercurrent of seriousness in what he said.

"One of those *what?*" Janet snapped. She glanced in alarm from Eric to Joe and then to the twins. "I'm not—*boring!*"

"Oh, really?" Joe held his head at an angle and stared at Janet, a trace of a smile on his face. "Could have fooled me."

"If you don't want one, Janet, I'll eat it," Jessica piped up. Grinning at Elizabeth, she started toward the couch. "*I'm* not one of those boring girls, that's for sure."

"And neither am I," Elizabeth chimed in.

Janet blinked hard. "Oh, *Eric*," she said in a despairing voice. "Please don't—"

"Don't what?" Eric narrowed his eyes and frowned at Janet. With a sudden motion he reached for the coffee can. "I don't want to make you do anything you don't want to do," he said levelly. "I just thought—well. Forget it. I guess I shouldn't have come over today, huh?" His fingers touched the edge of the can.

"Oh, don't do that!" Janet pushed Eric's arm out of the way. There was a long pause. "I mean . . ."

Eric made an impatient gesture. "Look, do you want one or not?" he demanded.

Janet looked like she might burst into tears. "All right," she said grudgingly, taking a long, shuddering breath. "They look so good. I'll—eat one."

"Yeah?" Joe raised his eyebrows. "Show us."

Janet smiled the tightest smile Elizabeth had ever seen. Almost mechanically she grabbed a cookie and thrust it between her jaws. Elizabeth's mouth watered. It *did* look good. Slowly, deliberately, almost painfully, Janet's front teeth closed on a piece of the cookie and forced it down her throat. "It's, um, delicious," she said in a choked voice.

"All right!" Joe shouted, pumping his fist. Elizabeth slapped five joyfully with her sister. *Yes!* she thought. It felt as if a great weight had just been removed from her shoulders.

"Huh?" Eric stared around the room, confused. "What's going on here?"

As one person, Joe, Jessica, and Elizabeth stretched out their forefingers to Janet.

"*Zap!*" they shouted in unison while Janet sank into the couch, a look of utter despair on her face.

So it all worked out, Joe thought, a grin on his face. He set a bowl of chips on the living room table and placed a jar of salsa next to it. Sure, he was going to have to wear a diaper tonight, but that was OK. After all, so was everybody else. Practically everybody anyway. Steven was going to have to wear one, courtesy of the twins. And Janet—well. His grin grew wider.

It had been a stroke of brilliance to call Eric, to tell him how much Janet would appreciate a gift of cookies while she was busy decorating for the party. He'd figured Janet wouldn't be able to say no to her new sort-of boyfriend. Especially not in front of the Wakefield twins. And especially because he'd told Eric that there was a foolproof way to tell how much Janet liked a guy: if she'd eat the cookies he baked just for her.

Yup. Joe nodded vigorously. So Janet would be in diapers after all. And Patty would be there. As *his* guest. So what if he had to wear a diaper? Big deal. He'd just laugh it off. *"Oh, this?" he'd say with a confident chuckle. "I was just in the wrong place at the wrong time, that's all." Then he'd motion to Janet and Steven and say, "Just like some other people I could mention . . ."*

Whistling happily to himself, Joe grabbed a stack of paper cups and put them by the lemonade pitcher.

"So I guess we won," Jessica said, beaming from ear to ear.

"I guess we did," Elizabeth agreed.

"It'll be fun seeing everybody *else* in those diapers," Jessica added. *Especially Janet. And Steven.* It was five o'clock. The twins had gone home to change after the decorations had all been hung, and now they were walking back up the Howells' driveway. On the horizon Jessica could see the sun just beginning to set.

"It sure will." Elizabeth paused on the front steps before ringing the doorbell. "So where are they?"

"Who?" Jessica frowned. "You mean the other guests?"

Elizabeth shook her head impatiently. "Not *who*, Jess. *What*. Where are the diapers?"

"The diapers?" Jessica narrowed her eyes and stared hard at her sister. "Why are you asking me? *You* were going to bring them."

"Me?" Elizabeth touched her chest. "Not *me!*"

"Yes, you were!" Jessica rolled her eyes. *Sisters.* "Don't *lie*, Elizabeth." A sudden thought seized her. "Don't tell me you've forgotten them?"

"How could I have forgotten them if I never knew I was supposed to bring them in the first place?" Elizabeth snapped. "Honestly, Jess, you're acting like—"

Jessica clenched her fists. "Don't be a doofus," she said through tight lips. She could feel her body beginning to tense. How could Elizabeth be so stupid? "You didn't think that Maria or *Amy* was bringing them, did you? Or *Janet?*" She spat out the last word as if it had a disease. "They lost, OK? *They're* not bringing any diapers along."

"I *know* that." Elizabeth folded her arms and glared at her twin. "I never said they were. It's just that . . . that . . . Steven told me *you* were bringing the diapers, and—"

"*Steven* told you?" Jessica gave a short barking laugh. "And you *believed* him? You're even stupider than I thought! Because it so happens that—"

"Me? Stupid?" Elizabeth set her jaw. "Talk about stupid! You don't even know iron pyrite from sulfur!"

Jessica shaded her eyes against the setting sun. "Like I *care!*" she jeered. "Anyway, for your information, Steven told *me* that *you* were bringing the diapers!" She could hear his voice echoing in her head. *"Elizabeth says she's got the diaper situation under control, kid,"* he'd said just after they'd gotten home from the Howells'. Then he'd put on this sad look and added, *"Too bad for me. You'd probably forget, but Elizabeth won't."*

"Typical." Elizabeth sniffed. "For your information—"

All the anger Jessica had been storing up for the last week came tumbling out. "I'm so *sick* of you!" she snapped, feeling her blood beginning to boil. "This week has been, like, the worst of my life, and it's all because of—"

"Don't you think I feel the same way?" Elizabeth stepped so close to Jessica that their noses were almost touching. "All week long it's been 'blah blah blah blah blah blah blah, you're so *stupid*, Elizabeth!'" Her eyes flashed, and her voice soared up to a mocking pitch. "Well, I'm tired of it too! I wish you would just—"

"Oh, shut up," Jessica ordered. If looks could kill, her sister would be stir-fry by now. "I'm—I'm *through* with you, Elizabeth! We won't get to see everybody in a diaper, and it'll be all your fault!"

"You mean *your* fault," Elizabeth snarled.

The sunlight flickered and dimmed. Jessica barely noticed. "Just get out of my life!" she yelled at the top of her lungs. "Just get out of my *life*, Elizabeth!"

"And you do the same thing!" Elizabeth tensed her neck muscles.

There was a sudden scrabbling in the bushes. Surprised, Jessica swung around.

Steven's head popped up. A grin was on his face. "Just under the wire," he said proudly, and he stretched out his forefinger at the girls.

"*Zap!*" he shouted.

"Two confirmed kills for Steven Wakefield!"

Thirteen

"No diapers, I see," Mrs. Wakefield said with a smile as the twins entered the Howells' house, Steven hot on their trail. Mr. and Mrs. Wakefield had come over earlier to have supper with the Howells—something about eating healthier food than chips and salsa, Elizabeth remembered. "So does this mean you all passed your New Year's resolutions?"

"Well—" Elizabeth blushed and looked at the ground.

"Sort of." Jessica rubbed her ear.

"As a matter of fact—" Steven broke off.

"Was there a problem?" Mr. Wakefield raised an eyebrow. He picked up a chip, dipped it gingerly into the salsa, and snapped off a bite. "I could get used to this every day," he said with a sigh. "Who cares about health anyway? Listen—what exactly do you three mean?"

"Um—" Jessica bit her lip.

Steven cleared his throat. "You see—"

Elizabeth took a deep unhappy breath. If it hadn't been for Steven tricking them about who was bringing the diapers. If it hadn't been for Jessica acting so mean. If it hadn't been for . . . She swallowed hard.

If it hadn't been for me either, she thought sadly. *If I hadn't believed Steven. If I hadn't snapped back at Jessica . . .*

Mrs. Wakefield searched the twins' faces. "Well?" she asked.

A sigh escaped Elizabeth's lips. "We didn't *exactly* keep our resolutions," she admitted. *Good-bye, ski trip.* "We tried, but it just . . . didn't work."

"Elizabeth!" Jessica sounded scandalized.

"I'm sorry, but I have to tell the truth!" Elizabeth burst out. "We really, really tried, but we couldn't do it. And the worst of it is . . ." She shook her head. "We could have done it, only . . . we wouldn't *let* each other do it."

Mr. Wakefield frowned. "What do you mean by that?"

Elizabeth screwed up her eyes. "Steven could have kept his resolution," she admitted in a small voice. "Except that . . . we . . . I . . . tricked him into watching TV." *There. I said it.*

"Tricked?" Mrs. Wakefield looked from Steven to Elizabeth and back.

"Tricked." Elizabeth felt about two inches high, but all the same it was good to get it off her chest. "We made up a story . . . about a videotape that we thought he'd want to watch . . . and—" She licked her lips nervously. "We, like, made a trap so he'd watch and break his resolution."

"I see." Mr. Wakefield shook his head sadly.

Steven rested his chin in his hands. "And I guess I'd better tell the truth too," he said unhappily. "The twins would have held it together also, but . . . well . . . I messed them up. And it wasn't, like, my first try either."

"I guess we really blew it," Elizabeth said thickly. "If you want to, you know, send us home from the party . . . I guess you could."

Mr. Wakefield rubbed his chin. "So all week long you've been working against each other."

Three heads nodded.

"Obviously none of you can be trusted to be at the ski condo without us," Mrs. Wakefield said. "I suppose we've learned that this week."

Elizabeth sighed and nodded again. Beside her Steven and Jessica were doing the same.

"They need supervision, Ned," Mrs. Wakefield said to her husband. "That's clear. I suppose that the decision we made today was the right one."

"De-Decision?" Jessica asked blankly.

"Aunt Nancy called," Mrs. Wakefield explained. "They'd invited some other friends to come along on their ski trip, but those friends had to cancel. So it seems that they have an extra double bed, and they asked if we wanted to come."

Elizabeth stared. "You?" she asked. "You mean, like—you two?"

"Yeah, *us* two," Mr. Wakefield said with a smile. He dipped another chip into the salsa. "We ski too, you know."

"At first we thought we wouldn't go," Mrs. Wakefield said. "It'll be hard to get away that week. But then I thought maybe we should go anyway. Maybe you kids shouldn't be away from us for a whole seven days."

"Besides, we *wanted* to go skiing," Mr. Wakefield put in.

"So we said yes." Mrs. Wakefield smiled. "And I guess that was the right choice. Sounds like you really aren't to be trusted yet, but we don't have to take away the trip altogether. You'll just have to put up with us."

Elizabeth relaxed. "Put *up* with you?" she asked, grinning at her sister and her brother. She could put up with anything as long as the trip was still on. Quickly she seized her family into a big hug. Even Steven. And even Jessica.

"I think we can put up with that," she murmured happily.

*   *   *

"I had more kills than anybody else," Janet boasted. "So I'm the winner." She reached for another one of Eric's chocolate chip cookies. "Speaking of kills, these are *killer* cookies."

"You *wish* you were the winner," Lila said haughtily. "Actually *I'm* the winner because I was out first. I got to spend the rest of the week watching you guys do silly things. It was like that show *Totally Cool Home Videos*. Wish I'd had a camera."

"What's this about *Totally Cool Home Videos*?" Steven asked plaintively. He shoved a huge wad of pretzels into his mouth. "Hey, Joe, turn on the TV. We're missing something really good, I can tell."

Jessica couldn't help a snort. *When some people break a resolution—they really break it!* she thought, feeling just a twinge of guilt. She sipped a cup of punch and stared morosely over the snack table. She ought to be happy, she knew. They were getting to go skiing, and nobody had to wear a diaper . . . but somehow . . .

"So, um—Jessica?" Elizabeth appeared at Jessica's elbow. She grinned weakly at her twin. "I think maybe we should, you know, talk."

Talk. Jessica nodded slowly. "I think so too," she said. "You first."

"No, you first," Elizabeth said quickly.

Jessica scowled. "No, *you* first—" She broke off suddenly. No. That wasn't the way to do it. Not at all. Taking a deep breath, she fumbled for Elizabeth's hand. "Listen, Lizzie," she said, not quite meeting her twin's eyes. "I'm—you know, sorry."

Elizabeth swallowed. "I know," she said gently. "So—am I."

A rush of relief swept through Jessica. She gripped her twin's hand tighter. "I guess I've been really obnoxious," she said with a low laugh. "I know it hasn't been exactly easy for you, having to put up with me."

Elizabeth smiled, and the twins' eyes met for an instant. "Me too," she said. "And you know what's so weird, Jess? I can be mean and nasty to anybody else, even Steven, and it doesn't bother me. Not all that much anyway," she added quickly. "But when I'm mean to you, it's like—well . . ." Her voice trailed off.

Jessica could feel tears welling in her eyes. "I know," she said. "You don't have to say it." Gently she tucked her arm around Elizabeth's shoulders.

"But I will anyway." Elizabeth's body trembled beneath Jessica's arm. "It bugs me when I'm mean to you because . . . because you're my very best friend in the whole world. And I really love you a lot, Jess."

"Same here." Jessica hugged her sister tightly, then released her. It was amazing how much better she felt. And when all was said and done, Elizabeth was exactly right. Deep down they were best friends. And if they worked at it, they would always be that way. No matter what.

"Hey, Jessica! Great party, huh?" Eric Weinberg

appeared on the other side of the refreshment table.

Jessica's eyes sparkled. "So, um, you want to dance, Eric?" she asked brightly. "I know Janet, like, invited you and everything. . . ."

"Oh, I'll dance with you," Eric assured her. "Janet's cute and everything, but I'm way too young to be tied down." His dark eyes sparkled. "I danced with Jessica too—"

"Jessica?" Jessica raised her eyebrows inquiringly.

Eric laughed. "Sorry. I guess I meant Elizabeth. You guys still look exactly alike to me."

Jessica smiled and let him steer her onto the dance floor. "You'll figure it out," she assured him.

"It was kind of funny," Eric said as a new song began. "Patty was sitting at home expecting your brother to call her and guess what? Joe invited her instead. Weird, huh?" He jerked his thumb toward Patty, who was standing in the doorway talking excitedly to Joe. "Looks like they have a lot in common too."

"Well, with four kills I *should* be declared the winner," Janet was saying with a shrug. "I mean, fair's fair and everything. . . ."

Good old Janet. Jessica grinned. She caught sight of Maria, Amy, and Elizabeth chatting on the couch. In the background her parents watched, smiles on their faces. Jessica took a deep breath. Everything was back to normal. Even though the resolutions hadn't quite worked out the way she'd hoped, she realized that she really couldn't be happier.

We're all having a great time, she thought as she whirled through the room, faces flashing by.

And best of all—no one has to wear a diaper!

Find out what happens when Elizabeth and Jessica are selected to be on Young Love, *the hottest new dating game show on TV, in Sweet Valley Twins #113:* The Boyfriend Game.

Bantam Books in the SWEET VALLEY TWINS series.
Ask your bookseller for the books you have missed.

SIGN UP FOR THE SWEET VALLEY HIGH® FAN CLUB!

Hey, girls! Get all the gossip on Sweet Valley High's® most popular teenagers when you join our fantastic Fan Club! As a member, you'll get all of this really cool stuff:

- Membership Card with your own personal Fan Club ID number
- A Sweet Valley High® Secret Treasure Box
- Sweet Valley High® Stationery
- Official Fan Club Pencil (for secret note writing!)
- Three Bookmarks
- A "Members Only" Door Hanger
- Two Skeins of J. & P. Coats® Embroidery Floss with flower barrette instruction leaflet
- Two editions of *The Oracle* newsletter
- Plus exclusive Sweet Valley High® product offers, special savings, contests, and much more!

Be the first to find out what Jessica & Elizabeth Wakefield are up to by joining the Sweet Valley High® Fan Club for the one-year membership fee of only $6.25 each for U.S. residents, $8.25 for Canadian residents (U.S. currency). Includes shipping & handling.

Send a check or money order (do not send cash) made payable to "Sweet Valley High® Fan Club" along with this form to:

SWEET VALLEY HIGH® FAN CLUB, BOX 3919-B, SCHAUMBURG, IL 60168-3919

NAME_____
(Please print clearly)

ADDRESS_____

CITY_____ STATE _____ ZIP_____
(Required)

AGE_____BIRTHDAY_____ /_____ /_____

Offer good while supplies last. Allow 6-8 weeks after check clearance for delivery. Addresses without ZIP codes cannot be honored. Offer good in USA & Canada only. Void where prohibited by law.
©1993 by Francine Pascal   LCI-1383-123